AF820250

A SERVING OF HOPE

Hisashi Kashiwai was born in 1952 and was raised in Kyoto. He graduated from Osaka Dental University. After graduating, he returned to Kyoto and worked as a dentist. He has written extensively about his native city and has collaborated on TV programmes and magazines.

Jesse Kirkwood is a literary translator working from Japanese into English. The recipient of the 2020 Harvill Secker Young Translators' Prize, his translations include *The Kamogawa Food Detectives* by Hisashi Kashiwai, *Tokyo Express* by Seicho Matsumoto and *A Perfect Day to Be Alone* by Nanae Aoyama.

Also by Hisashi Kashiwai

The Kamogawa Food Detectives
The Restaurant of Lost Recipes
The Menu of Happiness

A Serving of Hope

HISAHI KASHIWAI

Translated from the Japanese by Jesse Kirkwood

MANTLE

First published in the UK 2026 by Mantle
an imprint of Pan Macmillan
The Smithson, 6 Briset Street, London EC1M 5NR
EU representative: Macmillan Publishers Ireland Ltd, 1st Floor,
The Liffey Trust Centre, 117–126 Sheriff Street Upper,
Dublin 1 D01 YC43
Associated companies throughout the world

ISBN 978-1-0350-6076-4 HB
ISBN 978-1-0350-6078-8 PB

Copyright © Hisashi Kashiwai 2026
Translation copyright © Jesse Kirkwood 2026

The right of Hisashi Kashiwai to be identified as the
author of this work has been asserted in accordance with
the Copyright, Designs and Patents Act 1988.

Originally published in Japan as *Kamogawa Shokudo Omakase* by Shogakukan in 2017.
Japanese/English translation rights arranged with Shogakukan through Emily
Books Agency Ltd and Casanovas & Lynch Literary Agency SL.

All rights reserved. No part of this publication may be reproduced,
stored in a retrieval system, or transmitted, in any form, or by any means
(including, without limitation, electronic, mechanical, photocopying, recording
or otherwise) without the prior written permission of the publisher.

Pan Macmillan does not have any control over, or any responsibility for,
any author or third-party websites (including, without limitation, URLs,
emails and QR codes) referred to in or on this book.

1 3 5 7 9 8 6 4 2

A CIP catalogue record for this book is available from the British Library.

Typeset in ITC Galliard Std by Six Red Marbles UK, Thetford, Norfolk
Printed and bound in the UK using 100% Renewable Electricity by CPI Group (UK) Ltd

FSC
www.fsc.org
MIX
Paper | Supporting
responsible forestry
FSC® C116313

This book is sold subject to the condition that it shall not, by way of
trade or otherwise, be lent, hired out, or otherwise circulated without
the publisher's prior consent in any form of binding or cover other than
that in which it is published and without a similar condition including this
condition being imposed on the subsequent purchaser. The publisher does not
authorize the use or reproduction of any part of this book in any manner
for the purpose of training artificial intelligence technologies or systems.
The publisher expressly reserves this book from the Text and Data Mining
exception in accordance with Article 4(3) of the European Union
Digital Single Market Directive 2019/790.

Visit **www.panmacmillan.com** to read more about
all our books and to buy them.

CONTENTS

Chapter 1:
Miso Soup

1

There couldn't be many people who made it past thirty without ever visiting Kyoto, but Kenichi Yoshizawa was one of them. As he paced briskly north along Karasuma-dori, he found himself mentally comparing the city he knew so well from television and magazines with the one unfolding in front of him.

He'd had opportunities to travel in the past, but his studies had always come first. The idea of indulging in something as leisurely as a sightseeing trip – whether to Kyoto or anywhere else – had never even crossed his mind.

Kenichi had heard all about the city's scorching summers and freezing winters. What he hadn't expected was this clammy humidity, arriving before the rainy season had even set in. He took a handkerchief from his pocket and dabbed at his forehead.

Kyoto Tower. Higashi Honganji temple. The names

were familiar enough, but seeing them with his own eyes was something else. He felt a strange pang of nostalgia, as though he'd been reunited with an old friend.

From the central exit of Kyoto station, it took him ten minutes to reach a weathered two-storey building that matched the description he'd read. This had to be it. He slid the door open and called out, 'Hello?'

A young woman in a black sommelier apron turned towards him. 'Good afternoon!'

'Is this the Kamogawa Diner?'

'Well, yes,' she replied, eyeing him curiously.

Kenichi smiled with relief. He *was* in the right place, then. All that research had paid off.

A man dressed in a traditional, loose-fitting samue emerged from the kitchen. 'Here to eat?'

'Actually,' said Kenichi, producing his business card, 'I was hoping you might be able to track down a dish for me.'

'Ah.' The man passed the card to the young woman. 'My daughter handles that side of things.'

'*Gardenia Legal Services . . . Tokyo*,' she said, glancing up at him. 'Are you a lawyer?'

'Just a clerk at the firm. I'm still studying for the bar – though I know I look a little old for that.'

She gave a small nod. 'I'm Koishi Kamogawa, head of the Kamogawa Detective Agency. And this is my dad, Nagare, who runs the restaurant.'

Nagare removed his cap and bowed politely before setting it back on his head. 'You must be hungry. If you don't mind having the set menu, I can bring it out right away.'

Kenichi's expression brightened. 'That'd be wonderful.'

'Anything you're not so keen on?' Nagare asked.

'Well, I didn't grow up by the sea, so I've never been much of a fan of saltwater fish – mackerel, sardines, that sort of thing. Too oily for me. Otherwise, I'll eat anything. And I do love my vegetables.'

'Got it. I'll have something ready in a moment.' Nagare slipped past the noren curtain and into the kitchen.

'So how did you hear about us?' Koishi asked.

'I found you online. I searched for "food detectives". A few places came up, but yours seemed the most reliable.'

'Well, how about that . . .' Koishi grinned as she showed him to a table. 'I guess we must be famous. So – you're a fan of vegetables?'

'My family runs a farm. You could say I was raised on them.' Kenichi sat on one of the folding chairs and glanced around the restaurant.

Koishi's face lit up. 'A farm? Sounds idyllic.'

'It's probably not quite how you're picturing it. When I think of home, all I see is my mother scrabbling about in the dirt in her overalls.' He wiped the sweat from his neck with a hand towel.

'Thanks for waiting,' said Nagare, arriving with the food on a silver tray.

'Something to drink?' Koishi asked. 'We have all sorts.'

'I'm not much of a drinker,' Kenichi said, 'but I *am* thirsty. A beer would be perfect.'

'Draft or bottle?' asked Nagare.

'One of the small bottles, if you have them.'

'Of course.' Nagare hurried back to the kitchen.

'The humidity can be unbearable at this time of year,' said Koishi, pulling a white towel from her pocket and dabbing at her brow. 'Once it gets sticky like this, you know the heat is here to stay.'

'I used to complain about the cold winters back home,' Kenichi said, pressing his own towel to his neck again as he eyed the food on the tray. 'This is almost making me miss them.'

'Shall I give you a quick run-through?' asked Nagare, returning to his side.

Kenichi leaned forward. 'Please.'

'As Koishi was saying, Kyoto can get quite muggy at this time of year, which doesn't exactly do wonders for the appetite. But there are also plenty of ingredients that are at their best right now, and those are what I've focused on here. In the glass bowl in the top left is ayu sashimi – segoshi-style, with the soft bones left in – dressed with myoga ginger and perilla. Try it with the vinegared miso or the wasabi soy sauce. Alongside that is hamo eel tempura, served with curry salt. The small Karatsu plate on the right is lightly seared Omi beef, paired with an amanatsu ponzu sauce for a citrus kick. If you like, you can add a little grated garlic to the ponzu. On the left of the middle row is steamed pork – try that with the Korean-style sweet-and-spicy sauce, or just the mustard soy sauce if you want to keep things simple. In the Koimari bowl in the centre is the uzaku: grilled eel and finely sliced Kema cucumber tossed in black rice vinegar. On the right is a mini beef cutlet sandwich, made with lean Ishigaki beef. The bottom row is a Kyoto vegetable salad, though I've never been entirely sure what qualifies as a Kyoto vegetable. Greens, onions and root vegetables from a farmer I know, dressed with sesame sauce and chopped shibazuke pickles. Sprinkle a little ichimi pepper over it if you like. And instead of rice today, I'm serving a sobagome-zosui, a sort of buckwheat porridge. Just let me know when you'd like me to bring that out.'

With a smile, Nagare returned to the kitchen, Koishi following close behind.

Alone in the dining area, Kenichi sipped his beer and wondered where to start.

After trying a bit of the salad, he set his chopsticks down. 'Kyoto vegetables, eh . . .'

He reached for a piece of ayu sashimi, dipped it in the

vinegared miso and slipped it into his mouth. It tasted so unlike anything he'd ever eaten that he wasn't sure what to make of it. Maybe people thought of this sort of thing as a delicacy, but it wasn't the kind of flavour that left him craving more.

Then again, he'd never been that interested in food. Maybe it was only natural that he had no idea how to judge it.

'How is it, then?' asked Nagare, who had arrived at his side.

'It's delicious,' Kenichi replied tactfully.

'Glad to hear it.' Nagare glanced at the empty bottle. 'Another beer?'

'No, thank you. Think I've had enough.'

'Alright then. Just let me know when you're ready for the buckwheat porridge.' The chef slipped back through the curtain with the empty beer bottle. Kenichi watched him leave, then reached for the cutlet sandwich and took a bite.

'Wow,' he murmured.

The meat was just the right firmness, releasing a rush of rich juices as he chewed. The lightly toasted bread was the perfect match for the cutlet, and a ketchup-style sauce tied it all together. Nagare had said it was Ishigaki beef – from Okinawa, then. But the bread: was it just ordinary shop-bought bread? Kenichi felt a sudden wave of curiosity about the food in front of him. He chewed slowly, tilting his head from side to side, bewildered by the change that had come over him.

Next he reached for the uzaku.

His late father had loved eel, but their hometown had never had a decent eel restaurant. Even after he fell ill, he would often ask for it, and Kenichi's mother would drive nearly an hour to a place near Zenkoji temple to buy kabayaki, eel grilled in a soy-based sauce. She would slice up one of their own cucumbers, mix it with thin strips of the eel, and dress it with sweet vinegar before setting it down in front of his father.

Out in the countryside, eel had been a rare and expensive indulgence. He remembered being allowed a single bite, but the faintly muddy flavour of freshwater eel hadn't exactly charmed his taste buds. The uzaku he was eating now, though, felt like an entirely different dish.

He decided to return to the Kyoto vegetables. He took a slice of the onion and ate it plain – and was astonished by its sweetness.

He'd eaten onions all his life, in endless stir fries, stews and salads. But no matter how they'd been cooked, they'd always just been . . . well, onions. Sharp, pungent and never like this. It was as sweet as fruit.

The vegetables of his childhood seemed to pale in comparison to these Kyoto specialties. In fact, as odd as it sounded, they were almost *too* delicious.

'Shall I bring that porridge through?' asked Nagare, returning with impeccable timing.

'Please.'

For what felt like the first time in his life, Kenichi found himself looking forward to the next dish.

As a child, he'd eaten soba almost every day. Not in the form of noodles, but as sobagaki, where the buckwheat flour was mashed into a ball. And that, too, he didn't remember ever particularly enjoying. The sticky texture, the slightly grassy aroma. Back then, soba had always felt like a symbol of his family's poverty, and to this day he couldn't quite bring himself to enjoy it.

'Here we go,' said Nagare, setting a small iron pot before him and lifting the lid.

Kenichi peered through the billowing steam. 'This is sobagome-zosui, then?'

'Have you heard of Iya, in Tokushima?'

'Yes. Famous for those vine bridges, isn't it?'

'That's right. That, and all those stories about survivors from the Heike clan who fled there after the Genpei War. They're said to have started the custom of eating soba grains whole. Having fled to the village of Higashi-Iya, and missing the capital of Kyoto terribly, they made this porridge for the New Year. The ingredients are simple enough: chicken breast, thinly sliced daikon radish and carrot, dried shiitake and a mitsuba garnish. It's the texture and aroma of the soba grains that really make the dish.'

Nagare smiled warmly. Kenichi reached for the porcelain spoon and stirred the porridge lightly. Then he scooped some up, blew on it and slid it into his mouth.

It didn't taste like poverty, that was for sure. Alternating between the large grains of buckwheat, the vegetables and the broth, he found that each spoonful tasted subtly different. Savouring a single bowl of porridge at such length wasn't something he'd ever thought possible. Once he'd finished the very last grain he set the spoon back down and, almost instinctively, joined his palms in gratitude.

'Can I get you another bowl?' asked Nagare, arriving from the kitchen with a tray.

'No, thank you.' Kenichi bowed from his seat. 'But that was incredible.'

'Well, once you've had a moment to digest, I'll show you through.'

'I'm ready now, if you don't mind. I don't want to keep Koishi waiting.'

'Not at all. I hope you don't feel rushed.'

'Actually, I can't remember the last time I lingered like that over a meal.'

Nagare turned to him with a smile. 'The best compliment a chef can get. This way, please.'

He guided Kenichi down a corridor leading to the rear of

the building. Its walls were lined with pinned photos, mostly of food. Nagare's creations, presumably.

'She'll take it from here,' said the chef. He opened a door at the end of the corridor to reveal Koishi waiting behind a low table. She had changed into a black trouser suit.

'Could you fill this out, please?' Koishi asked, handing him a clipboard as he sat down on the sofa opposite her. On it was a short form.

Kenichi leaned forward and, setting the clipboard down on the table, filled out the entire form in less than a minute.

'Let's see,' said Koishi, retrieving the clipboard. 'Kenichi Yoshizawa, age thirty. You work for a law firm, and you live in . . . Machida? Where is that again? Somewhere near Tokyo?'

'You sound like my mother,' replied Kenichi with a wry grin. 'No matter how many times I explain it to her, she never quite gets it.'

'Commuting into Shinjuku every day must be rough,' sighed Koishi. She had brought up a map on her tablet and was swiping around on it.

'When I first moved there from the countryside, it really wore me down, but I'm used to it now. And on an income like mine, it's not like living downtown is even an option.'

Koishi put the tablet down. 'So, what's the dish you want us to find?'

'Miso soup.'

'Okay. A special type of miso soup?'

'No. Just the ordinary kind.'

'And where did you have it?' asked Koishi, flipping open a notebook.

'At home. My mother used to make it for me.'

Koishi jotted this down. 'Ah. Can't beat your own mum's cooking.'

'She made me a bowl every morning, all the way up until the end of high school. Miso soup and rice.'

'That's what, twelve years? Sounds like real devotion.'

'Even longer, I think. She started making it for me when I was still in nursery school, though I'm a little hazy on the details.'

'So she'd get up early, make the miso soup, then head out into the fields. And your father?'

Kenichi dropped his gaze. 'He was quite frail, and couldn't really help out much on the farm. He was in and out of the hospital all the time.'

'What a job your mum must have had. I don't think I could manage . . . Now, what kind of miso soup are we talking about?'

'What . . . kind? Just regular miso soup.'

'But what sort of miso – red or white?'

'Well, it wasn't red, but it wasn't exactly white either. More of a yellowish colour.'

'I forgot to ask. Where exactly did you grow up?'

'A place called Obuse, in Nagano.'

'Ah, Nagano. Probably Shinshu miso, then.'

'You think?'

'Well, the colour would certainly match.' Koishi scribbled another note. 'You said your family ran a farm. What did you grow?'

'A mix of things. Mostly apricots, apples and chestnuts, from what I remember. My mother and the other local farmers would work from first thing in the morning until sundown.'

'You didn't grow any vegetables, then?'

'Not to sell. But we cultivated plenty for our own use – onions, potatoes, cucumbers, tomatoes, cabbages, leeks, you name it. My mother had this little patch she'd tend between stretches in the fields. She still sends me onions and potatoes, so I guess it must be going strong.'

'It sounds wonderful,' said Koishi, her gaze drifting into space. 'Harvesting whatever you like, whenever you like . . . I'd love to live that way.'

'I guess the grass is always greener,' Kenichi replied. 'I used to hate the countryside. Dreamed of a life in the city. Then I actually tried it, and found out it wasn't all it's cracked up to be.'

Koishi readied her pen once more. 'So, what did your mother put in the soup?'

'It was different every day. Mainly vegetables, but never exactly the same combination.'

'She tried to keep things interesting, then. Must have taken some doing!'

'I remember the ingredients changing from day to day, but not what they actually were. I was always in a rush in the morning. Didn't even finish the bowl most of the time.'

'Oh dear,' said Koishi in a gently chiding tone. 'After she'd got up early to make it for you?'

'I know. I guess I just wanted a few more minutes in bed.'

Koishi pursed her lips. 'So, a vegetable miso soup, possibly made with Shinshu miso. That's all we've got to go on.'

'Sorry to be so vague,' said Kenichi, bowing his head.

'So,' Koishi said, eyeing him evenly, 'you just want to taste your mother's miso soup again, and you don't mind which exact vegetables are in it?'

'Actually,' replied Kenichi quietly, meeting her gaze, 'I want to taste the soup she made me on the morning of the twentieth of March, twelve years ago. The day I left Obuse.'

'Right. You would have been . . . eighteen? Can you tell me more?'

'My father hadn't always struggled with his health.

Something happened to make him that way.' Kenichi's mouth tightened. Koishi leaned forward to listen. 'A friend tricked him into taking on this huge debt. Before he knew what was happening, everything he owned had been seized. All that was left was our little house and a small part of the farm. I was still in middle school, so I only know what my mother told me. The shock seemed to break him. After that he was constantly ill.'

'How awful,' said Koishi in a gentle voice.

'When I finished middle school, my teacher told me, "Your poor father. If only he'd had a decent lawyer, none of this would have happened." That stuck with me. I decided right then that I'd become a lawyer someday. So I could help people with no one else to turn to.'

Koishi nodded earnestly. 'You had plenty of motivation, then.'

'Honestly, up until then I'd been as lousy a student as they come. Being a lawyer seemed like a total pipe dream.'

'But once you got to high school, you threw yourself into your studies?'

Kenichi nodded. 'Like my life depended on it. I surprised even myself. In the end I still had to take a year off before university to prep for the entrance exam, but I made it into the law faculty I wanted. My parents cried when I told them.'

'All your hard work paid off,' said Koishi, her eyes glistening slightly.

'Well, it turns out the world isn't that simple. If I wanted to be a lawyer, I had to pass the bar after graduating – and year after year, I just . . .' Kenichi's voice faltered.

'I've heard it's pretty brutal,' said Koishi.

'That's putting it mildly. Sometimes I just feel like it might be beyond me.'

'I'm sure you'll get there in the end.'

'Actually, my grade this year was one of the worst yet,' said Kenichi, gnawing at his lip in frustration.

'So, you're hoping your mum's miso soup will remind you why you set out to become a lawyer in the first place?'

'Maybe . . . The truth is, I'm not really sure. Lately I've been wondering if it's worth grinding myself down like this. Part of me thinks I should go back home and help out on the farm.'

'Sounds like a tough call. I wish I knew what to tell you.'

Kenichi sat up slightly. 'If I can just taste that miso soup again, I feel like I'll finally know what to do.'

'That makes sense. But if you want to eat that exact soup, I think our only option will be to ask your mother. No one else is going to know.'

'No. Please, anything but that. She's sharp, you know. She'd see right through me. And then she'd tell me never to give up, like she always does.'

'Let me guess. You haven't been back to Obuse once since you left at eighteen?'

'No. I made a promise to stay away until I became a lawyer, and my parents supported it.'

'Right. But they must miss you terribly. Do you have any brothers or sisters?'

'Nope. It's just me.'

'Your poor parents! If I was you, I'd be on the first train home this summer.'

'Every year, around Obon and the New Year, I have the same thought,' Kenichi admitted. 'But I just can't do it.'

'It's sort of like a vow you've made, then?'

'Something like that. I'm not asking to come home covered in glory. I just can't bear the thought of going back there without achieving what I set out to do.' Kenichi's voice had dwindled to a murmur.

'Then maybe this miso soup really will be a turning point. We'll have to track it down for you!'

Kenichi bowed. 'I'm counting on you.'

'But if you don't remember what went into it, and we're not allowed to ask your mother, this is going to be tough. Unless we develop psychic powers, I just don't see how we're meant to crack the case.'

'Please. There has to be a way.'

'Well,' said Koishi, snapping her notebook shut, 'we'll

just have to leave it to my dad. Just . . . don't expect a miracle, okay?'

'So, get everything you needed?' asked Nagare as they returned to the dining area.

'Mostly,' replied Koishi, giving Kenichi a sidelong glance.

'Sorry to put you to so much trouble,' he said, bowing to them both. 'It's all just so vague in my memory.'

'Well,' said Nagare, folding up the newspaper he'd been reading, 'whatever it is you're looking for, we'll do our best to find it.'

Kenichi bowed again. 'Thank you very much.'

'Seriously, though,' said Koishi, 'I wouldn't get your hopes up.'

Nagare frowned at her. 'Someone sounds a little pessimistic.'

'Yeah, well, just wait till you hear how little we've got to go on.'

They told Kenichi to return two weeks later, explaining that he could pay for the meal and their services then. When he stepped outside, he almost tripped on the tabby cat lying by the entrance.

'Interesting spot for an afternoon nap,' he said, crouching to stroke the animal's head.

'That's Drowsy,' said Koishi. 'He really can sleep anywhere.'

Nagare, meanwhile, was eyeing the dark clouds gathering in the west. 'Looks like we're in for a shower.'

'Take an umbrella,' said Koishi, offering Kenichi a plastic one.

'Don't worry,' he replied as he got to his feet. 'I'll run as far as the underground walkway.'

'Take care!' Nagare called after him.

'You know, Dad,' said Koishi when they were back inside, 'I'm not sure two weeks is going to be long enough. We could spend years on this and still come up with nothing.'

'Is it really that hard?' asked Nagare, sitting at the counter.

Koishi sat next to him and opened up her notebook. 'The hardest yet.'

'His mother's miso soup, eh?' said Nagare, running a finger over her notes. 'Does sound tough.'

'The worst part is, we're not allowed to ask the one person who might be able to tell us.' Koishi propped her chin in her hands. 'And besides . . .'

Nagare glanced up from the notebook. 'What?'

'Part of me feels like we shouldn't solve this one. For Mr Yoshizawa's own sake.'

'You know what I always say, Koishi,' said Nagare, turning back to the notes. 'Our job is to find the food. What the client does afterwards is up to them.'

'What's Obuse like, anyway?' Koishi asked suddenly.

'Oh, it's nice,' said Nagare without lifting his gaze. 'Famous for chestnuts. Lots of charming old buildings.'

'Can I take this one, Dad?' She tugged lightly at his sleeve. 'I'm dying to see this farm of his.'

'Well, okay, but . . . are you sure you'll manage on your own? Don't you want me to come along?'

'I'm in the mood for a little solo trip.'

'This isn't a holiday, you know. It's work.'

'I know, I know. Oh, I can bring you back some chestnuts.'

'I'm beginning to regret this already.'

'I wonder if there are any hot springs nearby?' Koishi murmured. Watching her swipe away at a map on her tablet, Nagare let out a long sigh.

2

Now the rainy season really had set in. Almost every day passed in a blur of drizzle, and the skies above Kyoto were grey and forbidding. The patter of droplets on Kenichi's umbrella was gentle enough, but large, glistening puddles lined the pavement that led past Higashi Honganji temple.

Picking his way between them, he walked east down Shomen-dori. This being his second visit, he made the journey from the station to the restaurant with ease. He closed his umbrella, removed his trench coat and slid open the door.

'Welcome back,' Koishi greeted him cheerfully.

'Thanks for your message,' replied Kenichi, draping his coat over a chair. 'I've been looking forward to this.'

Koishi began dabbing at the coat with a towel. 'Really coming down today, isn't it?'

'Oh, don't trouble yourself over that cheap old thing.'

'You braved the weather, then?' asked Nagare, poking his head out from the kitchen.

Kenichi bowed slightly. 'Thank you for looking into this for me.'

'It was Koishi who worked the case. Came back with the goods, too.'

Nagare glanced at his daughter, who puffed her chest out slightly. 'I'm pretty sure I've worked it out – but if not, I apologize in advance.'

'No need for that,' said Kenichi with a composed smile. 'I'm just grateful for your efforts.'

'I take it you'll have some rice with the soup?' asked Nagare. 'And if it's your high-school days you're remembering, I should probably make it an extra-large portion.'

'That'd be perfect,' said Kenichi, his smile widening.

Koishi set a brochure on the table. 'Well, I visited the Yoshizawa Farm.'

'Oh,' said Kenichi, glancing at the brochure. 'They've . . . turned it into a tourist attraction?'

'Your mother did. I think she was hoping it would become one of Obuse's sightseeing spots.'

'I had no idea,' murmured Kenichi, opening and flipping through the brochure.

'She gave it her best shot, but it doesn't seem many tourists showed up. Instead it's turned into something of a hangout for elderly people from the neighbourhood.'

Kenichi set the brochure down and smiled ruefully. 'My mother really isn't cut out for business.'

'Here she is,' said Koishi. She took the brochure and pointed to a photo of a woman smiling beneath an apricot tree. 'Hanae Yoshizawa.'

'It's really her . . .' Kenichi tilted his head, as if trying to reconcile the photo in front of him with the image in his memory.

'Here we go,' said Nagare, arriving with two bowls on a tray.

'We'll talk more when you're done,' said Koishi as she set a Mashiko teapot and Tobe teacup down on the table before heading for the kitchen.

'The pickles are nozawana. Otherwise, it's just the miso

soup and rice. Enjoy,' Nagare said, before he too disappeared behind the curtain again.

Left alone, Kenichi drew a quiet breath, then removed the lid from the soup bowl.

Once the steam had cleared, he reached for the chopsticks and gently stirred the soup. It was exactly how he remembered.

He lifted a slice of thinly cut potato. It was so soft it was on the verge of falling apart, and the instant it touched his tongue it seemed to melt. Its earthy sweetness was balanced beautifully by the savoury miso flavour that had permeated it.

At the bottom of the bowl, he could see thin translucent slices of onion. These, too, had been cooked right through, and practically dissolved in his mouth.

He lifted the bowl and sipped the broth.

'This is it,' he said, the words slipping almost unconsciously from his lips.

The miso was neither too harsh nor too sweet. Its soft, rounded flavour spread gently from his tongue to his throat, then settled in his stomach.

Now his eyes fell on the mound of rice in the indigo-patterned bowl. Taking a strip of the pickled nozawana, he curled it around the white grains and brought them to his mouth.

Memories were beginning to stir inside him. He lifted

the soup bowl once more and inhaled the steam. It was the exact aroma that had filled his nostrils on those bleary school mornings.

He reached for more slices of potato and onion, laying them gently on his tongue before sipping the broth. After doing this a few times, he reached for the rice bowl and, as if it were the most natural thing in the world, tipped its remaining contents into the miso soup.

He gave the bowl a quick stir, raised it to his lips and began slurping down the mixture of rice and soup, guiding the larger ingredients into his mouth with the chopsticks. In almost no time at all, the bowl was empty.

'How was it?' asked Nagare, returning from the kitchen with the tray.

'That was it, alright,' replied Kenichi, still cupping the bowl in both hands. 'My memories are still hazy, so it's hard to be certain, but something tells me that was the exact soup I had that day.'

'Can I get you some more?'

'No, thank you. I'm full – and I don't just mean my stomach. I feel like I have plenty to think about.'

'Glad to hear it. I'll bring you a cup of hojicha.'

'How did you . . . ?' Kenichi called after him.

'I'll let Koishi explain that part,' replied Nagare with a grin before disappearing through the curtain. Moments later, his daughter appeared in his place.

'I'm glad we got it right,' she said.

'Thank you. You're the one who cracked the case, then?'

'Mind if I sit?'

'Please.'

'I was expecting a challenge,' she said, joining him at the table, 'but when I got to Obuse it turned out to be easier than I expected.' She angled her tablet towards him and showed him a photo.

'Is that the community hall?'

'That's the one,' Koishi replied. 'Volunteers run an event there twice a week called the Silver Diner. A sort of lunch programme for senior citizens. And the miso soup there is in serious demand.'

'Wait. Is my mother the one making it?'

'That's right. They told me Hanae Yoshizawa was in charge of the miso soup.'

'So . . . the soup you just served me . . .'

'All the old gents there seem to have a soft spot for it.'

Kenichi stared down at his bowl in silence.

'They serve a few different versions on a rota,' Koishi continued. 'But this one, with just potatoes and onions, is the runaway favourite. I was informed it was Hanae's son's favourite, too.'

'You . . . didn't tell her about me, did you?'

'No, I heard that part from one of the regulars. An elderly

man who said he looks forward to it every time. Don't worry, I didn't tell your mother why I was there.'

'So the locals still remember me,' said Kenichi glumly.

'Of course they do! They're all wondering when you'll finally come home.'

'See, that's exactly what I can't stand,' said Kenichi. 'People in small towns don't realize the pressure they're putting on you. They think that as long as they're rooting for you, you're bound to return a winner. The local boy made good. But most of us don't. We come back with our tail between our legs, and all we want is to be left alone.'

'Do you think that's what it's all about? Winning?' said Nagare, appearing from the kitchen with a fresh pot of tea.

'It sure looks that way from where I'm standing. I went to Tokyo to make it as a lawyer, fell flat on my face, and now I'm going to have to return home a failure.' He gave a weak smile, and turned back to Koishi. 'You have to admit it's a little pathetic.'

'Listen, by your logic, I'm not much of a success either,' she replied, holding his gaze. 'Well into my thirties, and still living with my dad. But something tells me life isn't black and white like that. Whether you pass or fail the bar exam doesn't have to define you.'

'Sure, but . . .'

'How about we get back to that miso soup?' cut in

Nagare, noticing the uncertainty that had crept into Kenichi's expression.

'Right. The most important part.' Gathering herself, Koishi returned to the topic of the Yoshizawa Farm. 'I told your mother I ran a little restaurant in Kyoto and was desperate to learn the secret behind her soup. It wasn't exactly a lie, though I still felt pretty guilty about it.'

'She's always been the trusting type,' said Kenichi, wincing slightly. 'I bet she told you right away.'

'She's a lovely woman. I could see why the whole town would be charmed by her. She laid it all out for me – the specific blend of miso she uses, the exact balance of ingredients, everything.'

'So . . . that's how you managed it.' Kenichi was gazing at the bowl with an intensity bordering on reverence.

'Actually,' said Koishi, 'the soup I just gave you isn't quite the same as the one at the Silver Diner.'

'How do you mean?'

'I made the same assumption at first – that the soup those elderly gentlemen crave so much was the one you remembered from that morning. But as I was leaving, your mother showed me this.'

She placed an old, faded book on the table.

'*A Miso Soup for Every Day of the Year* . . .' Kenichi read aloud. 'A whole book about miso soup?'

The cover showed a turnip with its vibrant green leaves

still attached, set against the grooved clay of a traditional mortar for grinding. On the rear was a picture of a daikon radish, together with the book's price: a mere 380 yen.

'Published in the autumn of 1959,' Koishi explained, gently smoothing the creased cover. 'Your mother said she turned to these pages every single morning, so that your miso soup would be just right.'

'It's a fine book,' said Nagare, scanning the table of contents. 'And I don't just mean the recipes. The author gives you a sense of what cooking's really all about. It'd probably still sell today.'

'When I started copying out the bits that seemed useful, she insisted I borrow it,' said Koishi. She turned the book towards Kenichi, who began inspecting it. 'Look at the notes in the margins. Here: *Finished the whole bowl.* Or here: *Only had half.* Or this one: *Said it was tasty.* They're all about you.'

'She told you that?' Kenichi murmured, slowly leafing through the pages.

'Yes. She mentioned you because this was tucked between the pages.' Koishi set a photograph on the table. In it, a boy stood beside a woman in farming clothes. They were posing under a chestnut tree.

Kenichi reached for it immediately. 'This is that morning . . .'

'That's right. Taken the very day you left for Tokyo.'

'I remember joking that I might never come back,' said Kenichi, smiling softly. 'We both look a little anxious, don't we?'

'It's a lovely photo,' observed Nagare, peering over his shoulder.

'Once your name came up, she really opened up about the soup. I asked her everything I could think of.'

'She remembered the soup she made that day? After all these years?' asked Kenichi.

'Oh yes,' replied Koishi. 'Or rather, she had it all written down.' She pointed to a series of notes in the margins.

'*Blend Shinshu miso (three types)*,' read Kenichi. '*Just before it comes to a boil add pre-cooked onions and potatoes. Finish with a dash of Obuse milk*. Wait, there was milk in it?'

'That's what makes it different from the one at the Silver Diner,' Koishi explained. 'Your mother knew how much you'd loved milk as a little boy, so she always stirred a bit into the soup. Not just any milk, either. The local brand you'd grown up with.' She showed him a photo of a carton labelled *Obuse Milk*.

Kenichi's eyes crinkled as he smiled. 'I haven't seen that label in years.'

'It's a neat trick. Softens the sharpness of the miso,' Nagare commented. 'Your mother has chef's instincts.'

Koishi passed him a small paper bag. 'The miso blend and

recipe are in there. You'll have to source the milk yourself, though.'

'Thank you,' he replied. 'I'll be honest – I had my doubts that you'd actually pull this off. But this has . . . well, it's really helped me make up my mind.' A newfound determination had settled over his features.

'Glad to hear it,' said Nagare, smiling broadly.

Kenichi pulled out his wallet. 'Now, can I pay you for everything?'

'Just whatever you feel is fair,' Koishi said, handing him a note with their bank details.

Kenichi slid open the door and glanced up at the sky. Long shafts of sunlight were finally breaking through the clouds. Drowsy the cat was sprawled at the base of a utility pole, yawning lazily.

'Someone has the right idea,' observed Kenichi, his trench coat and umbrella tucked neatly under one arm.

'Do take care!' said Koishi, and they exchanged a bow.

'About this book,' said Nagare, turning the miso soup cookbook over in his hands. 'Your mother said we could borrow it until her son came home. And that she'd let us know when that was. Right, Koishi?'

Koishi nodded firmly.

'Funny,' said Kenichi. 'I feel like I've taken the long way round, somehow.'

Nagare smiled back at him. 'This is life we're talking about. It's not like there are any shortcuts.'

'I can't thank you enough.' Kenichi bowed again, deeply this time. Then he walked off down Shomen-dori the way he'd come.

'Is this one of those times when people say you need rain to make a rainbow?' said Koishi as they made their way back inside.

'Sure,' replied Nagare with a wry grin. 'Something like that.'

'I wonder what he'll do. Keep trying, or head home?'

'I imagine he'll do whatever feels right,' said Nagare, settling himself before the family altar in the tatami-matted living room that adjoined the kitchen. Koishi took her place beside him.

'Remind me, Dad. What did Mum like to put in her miso soup?'

'Poached egg,' said Nagare as he lit a stick of incense. 'She'd make plain miso soup, drop in a raw egg, then simmer it so that the white set but the yolk was still soft. She used to get so worked up if she overcooked it.'

'That's one of my favourites, too,' Koishi said softly, closing her eyes and pressing her palms together in prayer.

Chapter 2: Onigiri

1

The moment Shiori Yukimura stepped out of Kyoto station's central exit, she felt it in the air: the crisp chill of autumn. A faint shiver ran through her, and she looked down at her thin white dress with a sudden pang of regret.

Glancing up at Kyoto Tower, stark against a ceiling of grey cloud, she set off north along Karasuma-dori. She'd been told it was only a ten-minute walk to her destination. As she neared Higashi Honganji temple, she slowed her stride, letting its quiet atmosphere soak in before she turned east down Shomen-dori. Soon she had arrived at a mortar-walled building.

'Excuse me,' she said to the young woman crouching by the door with a tabby cat in her arms. 'Is this the Kamogawa Diner?'

The woman rose to her feet, the cat still tucked securely against her chest. 'That's us.'

'And . . . am I correct in thinking you offer a "food detective" service?'

'Ah. You're not just here for a meal, then.' The woman bowed politely. 'I'm Koishi Kamogawa, head of the Kamogawa Detective Agency.'

'Shiori Yukimura. I saw your advert in *Gourmet Monthly*.'

'Come on in.' Koishi set the cat down by the entrance and slid open the door.

As Shiori made her way inside, a man in a brown, loose-fitting samue and cap emerged from the kitchen and said, 'Hello there.'

'It's my dad here who does the real detective work,' explained Koishi, before turning to her father. 'This is Shiori Yukimura. She saw the magazine advert.'

'Pleasure to meet you.' Shiori bowed, sending her long black hair swishing across her pale face.

'Likewise,' said Nagare, removing his cap and bowing. 'Now, how's your appetite? I can serve you the set menu if you like.'

She beamed at him. 'Really? That'd be wonderful. Though I feel bad turning up out of the blue like this.'

'Anything you can't eat?'

'No. I . . . let's just say picky eaters were frowned on in my family.'

'Alright then. Just give me a moment.' Nagare strode back into the kitchen.

'Take a seat,' said Koishi, gesturing towards one of the folding chairs. Shiori did as instructed, glancing curiously around the restaurant.

'If you read *Gourmet Monthly*,' Koishi went on, 'you must be something of a foodie.'

'Actually, I came across it at my workplace. We always leave a copy out for customers.'

'Well, I'm amazed you found us from that one-line advert.' Koishi grinned cheekily. 'And I say that as the one who wrote it.'

'I took a chance and phoned the magazine directly. The editor-in-chief was kind enough to give me directions.'

'May I ask where you've come from today?'

'Tokyo. Though I'm originally from Murakami in Niigata.'

'Ah, Niigata. Some of the best rice and sake in the country, for my money.' As she carefully wiped down the laminated table, Koishi sneaked a glance at Shiori's impressive outfit.

'Thanks. People do say that. Though to be honest, when I lived there I didn't think much of the place.'

'Do you work in fashion, by any chance?'

Shiori's white dress, with its delicate pleating, looked especially striking in the modest surroundings of the restaurant.

'I'm a hair stylist, actually,' replied Shiori modestly. 'But I suppose it's a similar sort of world.'

'A hair stylist! When you mentioned customers just now, I pictured you working in some high-end clothing boutique. But hairdressing must be pretty glamorous, too.'

'I know it seems that way, but the truth is it's exhausting. We're on our feet all day long.'

'I'd never thought about that. The customers get to take it easy, while the staff run about tending to their needs . . . Sounds a bit like this place, actually.'

The pair exchanged a glance and laughed.

'Still,' said Shiori, 'it's the smile on the customer's face that keeps you going, isn't it?'

'Exactly,' replied Koishi. 'You know, I love getting my hair done. It's such a mood-booster. I used to dream of being a hairdresser.'

'Well, your hair looks great.'

Koishi hunched her shoulders bashfully. 'That's very kind of you. I'm never quite sure I'm styling it right.'

'Sorry to keep you waiting,' said Nagare, arriving with a long tray laden with food.

Shiori's eyes opened wide. 'Wow. What a spread!'

'We're at that funny in-between time, when summer's over but autumn isn't quite here yet, which means there aren't many big hitters on the menu. Still, I hope you'll enjoy the meal.' He arranged the dishes on the table, then went on. 'Let me run you through it. The long plate in the top left is salt-grilled ayu filled with roe. Try that with the yuzu miso. Next, in the Oribe bowl, you have the oboro tofu topped with fresh sea urchin. Perfect with a dab of kanzuri chilli paste. The blue-and-white porcelain bowl at the end is kumiage yuba – the delicate skin that forms on soy milk. That comes dressed in Tosa vinegar. The glass plate below it is parboiled hamo eel – try that with the plum vinegar or mustard miso, whichever takes your fancy. Next to that, in the steamer, are the squid shumai dumplings. Nice with the sesame paste and a bit of coriander. And to the left of that is the grilled autumn aubergine in a ginger glaze. On the bottom row, the square dish is simmered Omi beef, which goes very well with a dab of the mustard paste. Then you have the Tatsuta-style deep-fried venison, and finally anago eel steamed with a layer of cucumber. Those last two are already seasoned, so you can enjoy them just as they are.'

Having rattled through this monologue, Nagare looked to Koishi, who asked Shiori if she wanted anything to drink.

Shiori smiled back at her. 'With a feast like this, how could I not? Can you recommend a good sake?'

'Spoken like a true Niigata native,' said Koishi, nodding with approval. 'I guess when you're born in the homeland of sake, anything else is out of the question.'

Nagare gave an amused chuckle. 'Not sure about "homeland", but . . . Anyway, do you prefer it on the dry side?'

'Not one of those delicate tanrei ones everyone seems to be drinking these days. I prefer something with a bit more weight to it. I think I get that from my father. He was something of a sake fiend.' A faint shadow crossed Shiori's face as she said these last words.

'You're right. Tanrei seems to be all anyone talks about recently, but a lot of them are pretty characterless. I'll bring you something with a proper punch.' Nagare hurried off into the kitchen.

'So,' said Koishi conspiratorially, 'is it true that in Niigata, they get you started on sake when you're still a kid?'

Shiori smiled back at her. 'I'm not even sure how to answer that.'

'Koishi,' said Nagare, returning with a bottle of sake, 'if you keep chattering away like that, she won't be able to enjoy her meal.'

'Sorry. I let my curiosity get the better of me sometimes.' Koishi winced slightly as she returned to the kitchen.

'Not at all,' Shiori called after her. 'It's fun to chat.'

Nagare set the bottle down. 'This is Tenju, an Akita brew. I can warm it up for you if you like, but I'd recommend trying it at room temperature. It's been my go-to in the evenings lately. Anyway, enjoy the meal.'

He went back into the kitchen, and a pleasant silence descended over the restaurant. The first dish she reached for was the salt-grilled ayu. Back in Murakami, ayu had been a dinnertime staple in the summer, thanks to a neighbour who would catch them in the nearby Miomote River. Having grown up eating ayu so fresh her mother had to wrestle with the still-flopping fish to get the skewers in, she'd always been disappointed when she ate it at a restaurant. So it was without expecting much that she raised a morsel to her lips and began to chew.

'Wow,' she blurted, surprising even herself.

The fish's belly had split open as it was grilled, releasing its golden roe. She'd heard people say that, because all the nutrients went to the eggs, the flesh of late-season ayu lacked flavour. Now she knew how wrong they were. If anything, the taste seemed richer than that of young ayu caught in the spring, while the yuzu miso added a bright, citrusy aroma that really lifted the dish.

Next she turned her attention to the oboro tofu, adding a dab of kanzuri to the sea urchin on top. The sharp fermented heat of the chilli paste paired perfectly with the rich creaminess of the tofu, which practically melted in her mouth. It was a combination that stirred something inside her. Maybe that was because a jar of kanzuri had been a constant presence in her family's fridge. Whenever they'd wanted to spice something up, or boost or tweak a flavour, it had always been the kanzuri they reached for. It had gone into the dipping sauce for somen noodles and been slathered onto bowls of white rice; sometimes it had even been stirred into ramen. She'd had it with tofu plenty of times, but never with the addition of sea urchin.

Hamo eel, meanwhile, she knew as a Kyoto favourite – one that was usually in season in summer, around the time of the Gion Festival. She hadn't known you could even catch it in the autumn. She tried dipping it in the mustard miso. It tasted so good she almost groaned aloud.

She didn't remember ever trying venison before, but it turned out to be surprisingly easy to eat, probably because it had been deep-fried. Compared to something like chicken kara-age, the flavours seemed richer and deeper.

'Some more sake, maybe?' asked Nagare, appearing from the kitchen right on cue. She had just been thinking she could do with another drink.

'Please. Whatever you recommend.'

'Here's one from Omi I think you'll like. Has a nice sturdy flavour.'

As she worked her way through the dishes, Shiori felt the first prickles of anxiety. Was she really going to ask the person who had created these masterpieces to recreate something as simple as a rice ball? The mere thought made her flush with embarrassment.

Her family had never been very well off, and growing up in Murakami she'd only known modest food. To her parents food was sustenance, not something you indulged in. It was only after moving to Tokyo two years ago that her eating habits had undergone a shift; with a steady salary and countless top-tier eateries on her doorstep, she had reinvented herself as someone who appreciated the finer things. Without that time in the capital, the sheer artistry of Nagare's cooking would have been lost on her.

Savouring the Omi sake, which hit all her favourite notes, she polished off the rest of the meal. Nagare returned from the kitchen just as she was setting her chopsticks down.

'Here's the rice dish. I hope I'm not rushing you?'

'Not at all,' replied Shiori, wiping her lips with the damp oshibori. 'I don't want to keep Koishi waiting.'

'This is ayu rice. I grill the fish first, season it ever so slightly, then flake the flesh off and steam it with the rice. I have to admit I'm a little nervous serving rice to someone from Niigata.'

Nagare spooned rice from a round wooden container into a small bowl, which he placed in front of Shiori.

She might have been born in Niigata, but that didn't mean she grew up eating any of the prefecture's famous brands of rice. In fact, she'd never paid much attention to where it came from, though the rice they got from a local farmer had been undeniably tasty.

'It smells wonderful. Looks incredible, too.'

'Try topping it with some chopped perilla, myoga ginger, mitsuba and pepper tree leaves. The miso soup is with autumn aubergines. Enjoy!' Tucking the round tray under his arm, Nagare disappeared back into the kitchen.

Shiori's father had never cared much about the quality

of the rice, but he'd been very particular about how her mother cooked it. If it was even slightly too firm or too soft, he'd yell at her until he was red in the face.

A faint aroma of ayu drifted up from the bowl, but the rice was uniformly white in appearance. The fish had simply been mixed in with the rice; even when she tried a mouthful, it was hard to tell it was there at all. Then she added the perilla, mitsuba, myoga and pepper tree leaves, and everything changed. It was as though, all of a sudden, a fragrant breeze had come drifting towards her across a river.

Shiori thought back to the day when, sitting on the banks of the Miomote, she'd had her first real conversation with Yasuhiko Ono.

She had been eighteen, and he nineteen. Listening to Yasuhiko speak passionately of his dream of becoming one of Japan's top chefs, she had felt strangely embarrassed. She had no real dreams of her own, and had only started working at a local beauty salon because the pay and conditions were decent.

She recalled, as vividly as if it were only yesterday, the evening sun shimmering on the river's surface.

'Well?' said Nagare, appearing with a teapot. 'How was it?'

'Absolutely delicious,' she replied with simple sincerity.

'Good to hear. I'll show you through to the office when you're ready.'

'I'll see her now, then.' Shiori took a quick sip of the tea in her cup and, smiling, got to her feet.

The building was built in the old Kyoto style, often likened to that of an eel's bed: a narrow frontage concealing a deep interior that stretched back from the street. He led her down a corridor lined with photos. Almost all of them were of food.

'Are these all from the restaurant?'

'Just about, though there are a few family snaps in there too. I don't usually bother writing down recipes, so this is my way of keeping track.'

'You make all sorts, then – not just Japanese food. Where did you train?'

'My family ran a restaurant. My father was the second generation, and I was supposed to be the third. I never had what you'd call proper training, though – just sort of watched and learned. And to top it off I got sidetracked along the way.'

Nagare gave a rueful smile. Shiori wanted to ask what he meant by getting sidetracked, but he had turned away as if to signal that the conversation was over.

'Koishi will take it from here,' he said, opening the door at the end of the corridor.

Shiori stepped inside and sat on the sofa.

'It's a bit of a hassle, but could you fill this out?' Koishi handed her a form on a grey clipboard, on which Shiori scribbled her address, name, occupation and date of birth.

'So you're originally from Murakami, but these days you're based in Yoyogi?'

'That's right, I've been in Tokyo for two years now. Murakami feels further and further away with every passing day.'

Seeing the faint sadness that crossed Shiori's face, Koishi felt a twinge of envy. Born and raised in the city of Kyoto, she'd never had a rural hometown to pine for. Every year, her classmates would return from their summer holidays brimming with tales of rural adventures and eccentric grandparents – experiences she'd never known, and could only yearn for.

'So, what are you looking for?'

Shiori paused briefly before answering. 'Onigiri.'

'Onigiri? As in . . . a rice ball?' Koishi realized how idiotic her question sounded, but Shiori took it in her stride.

'That's the one.'

'Hmm. Dad always says simple dishes are the hardest to get right.'

'Sorry about that.'

'Oh, not at all,' said Koishi with a playful grin. 'He likes a challenge.'

'That's reassuring.'

Koishi flipped open her notebook. 'So, tell me all about it. When and where did you eat this onigiri, and what was in it?'

'It was the summer I turned twenty, so just over four years ago now.' Shiori paused and let out a soft sigh. 'After high school I took a job at a local beauty salon. The owner would sometimes take me out for dinner once we'd closed up. One night we went to Bettei Haguroan, a well-known local restaurant, and I happened to get talking to one of the apprentice chefs. We started seeing each other not long after that.'

'May I ask his name?' asked Koishi, her pen at the ready.

'Yasuhiko Ono.'

'And how old was he?'

'A year older than me,' replied Shiori, lowering her gaze.

'And . . . he made the onigiri?'

'Yes. We'd been together for over a year at the time.'

'And where did you eat it?'

'In Murakami, there's this park with a funny name: Salmon Park. It was summer – the night of Tanabata, in fact – and we'd met up after work.' A flush spread across Shiori's cheeks.

'A late-night date on Tanabata?' said Koishi, her eyes sparkling. 'How romantic.'

'He'd asked to talk. Said he had something important to tell me.'

'Ooh. Don't tell me he proposed.'

'The opposite. He said we shouldn't see each other for a while.'

'Oh . . . had he fallen for someone else?'

'No, nothing like that. He said he wanted to focus on his training. That once he'd become a fully fledged chef we could be together properly. It would take him about four years. He wanted to know if I'd wait.'

'Four years? That's a big ask. Not sure I'd have the patience.'

'I wasn't sure either. I mean, anything could happen in that time. What if one of us fell for someone else? I told him it wasn't a promise I could make.'

'I don't blame you. There's no telling what'll happen in one year, let alone four. It's like waiting for the next Olympics!'

Shiori chuckled at the comparison. 'He talked about how little he earned, how he couldn't even afford to take me out properly. He said he wanted us to live together right away, but not if it meant me suffering at the side of someone who could barely make ends meet.'

'He sounds like a man of principle,' said Koishi with a quiet sigh. 'Still – four years . . .'

'I told him he didn't have to take me out on fancy dates.'

'Exactly. Why does it have to be about spending money? Whatever happened to just going for a nice stroll in the park?'

'But I knew what he was like,' said Shiori, gazing absently

into space. 'Once he decided on something, that was it. He never backed down.'

'Stubborn to a fault, eh? Sounds just like my dad.'

'Anyway, there was a lull in the conversation, and then he brought out the onigiri. Told me he'd made it specially for me. It was in this beautiful wooden box.'

'A farewell onigiri? Hmm. I can't quite decide if that works.'

'I remember thinking it was just like him, somehow.'

Koishi flipped to a fresh page in her notebook. 'Tell me more about this onigiri.'

'Well, it was triangular, and a little bit smaller than the ones you get at convenience stores. It was wrapped in seaweed, and there were ingredients mixed in with the rice.'

'*Ingredients mixed in*,' Koishi murmured as she scribbled away. 'What sort of ingredients?'

'That's the thing. I couldn't quite tell. I do remember it tasting of fish, but beyond that . . .'

Koishi smiled gently. 'That makes sense. I don't think many people would be concentrating on the onigiri in that situation.'

'I broke it in half, glanced at the filling, then ate the whole thing right way.'

'How did it taste?'

'I'd never had anything quite like it. I remember thinking

it had a sort of . . . refined flavour. It was just an onigiri, but you could have paired it with a drink. It might have been minced fish, but it also tasted a bit like prosciutto or something.'

'Hmm,' said Koishi, cocking her head to one side. 'Not much to go on.'

'I'm not sure if this helps, but he mentioned that the filling was a very rare ingredient. One of their customers had cancelled at the last minute, and he'd been allowed to keep the unused food. He was very proud of that part.'

'That does sound like a useful detail.'

Shiori bowed her head apologetically. 'Sorry to be so vague.'

'So, what made you want to eat this onigiri after all this time?'

'I've met someone new.'

'I see. Well, four years have passed. And Yasuhiko hasn't been in touch?'

Shiori silently shook her head.

'Then what's the problem? You're young. Nothing wrong with falling in love again.'

'It's just that . . . well, before I move on, I'd like to taste that onigiri one more time. I want to know what was going through his mind when he made it.'

Shiori looked imploringly at Koishi, tears shimmering

in her eyes. It struck Koishi then just how deep her feelings for Yasuhiko must have been. Even after all this time, and without a word from him, she was still waiting. But if she didn't let go, she'd never find happiness. Koishi knew well – painfully well, in fact – what Shiori was going through.

'Alright,' she said, a fresh determination coming into her voice. 'We'll get to the bottom of this. If Dad can't, I will.'

'Thank you so much. I really do appreciate it.' Shiori stood up and gave a deep bow.

They returned to the restaurant to find Nagare busy prepping food.

'Did you get the whole story, then?' he asked, covering a metal tray with a lid.

'Just about,' replied Koishi. She lifted the lid and peered inside. 'What are you making?'

'Semi-dried venison. Another couple of weeks and it'll be perfect.' Nagare gazed at the dark red meat for a moment, then replaced the lid.

Koishi noticed Shiori staring at the tray, and asked, 'Something the matter?'

'That might have been what was in it . . .' she murmured, her eyes glazing over slightly.

'Venison? Dad, do they eat a lot of venison in Niigata?'

Nagare tilted his head thoughtfully. 'Can't say I've ever heard of anything like that. But who knows?'

'I'm probably just imagining things,' said Shiori. 'Now, when should I come back?'

'Give us two weeks,' said Koishi. 'I'll be in touch when everything's ready.'

'Got it. I work late, so you might have to leave a message on my voicemail.'

As Shiori stepped outside, a tabby cat came bounding over, and she crouched to stroke it. 'Your cat?'

'In a manner of speaking.' Koishi eyed Nagare reproachfully. 'Dad never lets him inside.'

'Of course I don't,' he retorted, folding his arms and looking to one side. 'You can't have a cat wandering around a place that serves food.'

'What's his name?'

'Drowsy,' said Koishi, squatting at her side. 'Mainly because he spends his whole life sleeping.'

'It's the same at my salon. The owner's wife has a cat, but he absolutely refuses to let it inside. They're always arguing about it.' Shiori rubbed Drowsy's neck, eliciting a friendly purr.

'Where are you heading now, then?'

'Back to Tokyo,' replied Shiori, rising and smoothing out her dress. 'I have work tomorrow.'

'Well, it looks like rain,' said Nagare, glancing up at the grey sky. 'Travel safe.'

Shiori thanked them again, then set off down Shomen-dori.

'So,' said Nagare after they'd seen her off, 'what's the dish?'

'An onigiri.'

Nagare went back into the restaurant and sank into one of the folding chairs. 'Hmm. Tough one.'

'Definitely. But at least we know who made it. If all else fails, we can always just ask him.' Koishi sat opposite him and showed him her notebook.

'Murakami, eh? Nice little town. Great sake and rice, and the fishing's good too.'

'Maybe I should take this one,' said Koishi.

'No way. An onigiri is high stakes, Koishi. I'll go myself.'

'Oh, come on. You just want an excuse to drink some good sake.'

'Nonsense. If you come back empty-handed, we'll have to start over. Listen, I'll bring you home a nice bottle of sake – just stay put and mind the shop.'

'Alright,' said Koishi, pouting slightly. 'But you'd better not forget that sake.'

2

In autumn, a lot can change in two weeks. The Kyoto air wasn't just chilly now, it carried a wintry sting. This time, though, Shiori had come prepared. She was wearing a thick jacket, and as she walked along Karasuma-dori she adjusted a beige scarf around her neck.

There were no brooding clouds this time, either; the sky was an unbroken expanse of blue. The white spire of Kyoto Tower loomed proudly over the streets.

As she turned onto Shomen-dori and came to a halt in front of the Kamogawa Diner, Shiori felt a strange rush of nostalgia, even though this was only her second visit. Maybe it was because she was reminded of the house where she'd grown up: a two-storey building whose grey mortared walls were veined with cracks. The cracks had been sealed with white filler, and as a child they had seemed to her the tentacles of some grotesque creature. She remembered rushing in without even daring to look at them.

Inside, Koishi greeted her with a bright smile.

'We've been looking forward to seeing you again,' said Nagare, dressed in his brown samue and a cap of the same colour, which he removed in order to bow.

'I've been looking forward to it, too.' Shiori made to remove her jacket, but Nagare held up a hand.

'Keep that on, please. I thought we could go on a little outing.' He nodded to Koishi, who produced a handwoven rattan basket. 'There's no Salmon Park in Kyoto, unfortunately, but there *is* a little garden just round the corner. It's a modest place, but I'd like to take you there. Onigiri always taste better in the open air.'

Shiori felt herself relax. She'd found it hard to imagine eating the onigiri within the confines of the restaurant. Nagare's suggestion made a lot more sense.

'It's a place called Shoseien,' explained Koishi while Nagare was getting things ready. 'Though the locals usually call it Kikokutei.'

'Right. And is it a . . . park?' Shiori was finding it hard to picture their destination.

'Sort of. It's actually part of Higashi Honganji, even if it's not on the same plot of land. The temple's garden, if you like.'

'Oh, that's the big temple I passed on my way here, right? It looked enormous.'

'The garden's a few minutes' walk from here. I drop by sometimes when I need to clear my head. There's something relaxing about being able to see so much sky.'

'Right,' said Nagare, having finished his preparations. 'Off we go!'

He led them east down Shomen-dori.

'See that gate?' said Koishi, pointing down the street. 'That's the entrance.'

'You weren't joking when you said it was close.'

'Now, this is a temple,' said Nagare as they reached the gate, 'so it's not like people are allowed to picnic on the benches. But you should be okay eating a rice ball by the pond.'

Shiori nodded, still trying to get her head around the idea that the garden was actually temple property.

At the entrance, Nagare paid for all three of them, motioning for Koishi and Shiori to follow him inside. Shiori noticed how the sign referred to a 'viewing fee' rather than an 'admission fee'.

The garden was bigger than she'd expected, with various structures scattered among the neatly tended trees. Nagare led them to a pond.

'It's not quite the fountain in Salmon Park, but if you sit here and gaze at the water while you eat, it should at least set the mood.'

The pond was small enough to take in at one glance but not so large as to be overwhelming. Kyoto Tower was reflected in its depths. Nagare had clearly scouted this location in advance. He strode over to a flat stone that looked perfect for sitting on.

'Maybe not the most comfortable seat in the world, but it

should do. And I brought this.' He produced a small indigo cushion and set it on the smooth dark stone.

'And here's the onigiri,' said Koishi, handing the basket to Shiori. 'There's a flask of tea in there as well.'

'Thank you so much.'

'We'll go for a little stroll, so take your time, okay?' Nagare nodded to Koishi, and the pair departed.

There was hardly anyone around. Glancing around the large garden, Shiori only counted a dozen or so people. Still, though she basically had the pond to herself, the knowledge that this was technically a temple made her slightly self-conscious about eating. She peered into the rattan basket, retrieved a small box, and carefully opened the lid.

Inside were two triangular onigiri that looked just like the ones she remembered. They were wrapped in nori, but the seaweed wasn't brittle or flaky like on convenience store onigiri. It was soft, moist and practically melded to the rice. She picked one of them up, gazed at it for a while, then brought it slowly to her lips.

Gently, carefully, she chewed on the rice. It was saltier than she'd expected, with an almost briny aroma that tickled her nostrils.

Yes, this was it. This was how it had tasted.

Holding the onigiri in one hand, Shiori stared down at the pond's surface, from which Yasuhiko seemed to gaze back up at her.

I'm used to scraping by, she'd wanted to tell him. *I've never wanted luxury. We could make it work. You might not earn much, but with my wages we'd have enough to live on. I could wait one year, maybe even two. But not four. I just want to be together.*

The words had been on the tip of her tongue, but she'd been scared. Scared that uttering them aloud would shatter the fragile future he'd so tenderly imagined for them.

As she slipped the last of the first onigiri into her mouth, tears began spilling down her cheeks.

She should have spoken her mind, even if it meant an argument. Even if it meant shattering that dream. Dreams could always be mended. But when she voiced these thoughts to Yasuhiko's wavering reflection in the pond, he simply stared back in silence.

She took the second onigiri from the box and broke it in half. The sticky, finely minced filling was a dark vermilion. When she bit into it, her mouth filled with that rich, briny aroma.

This time, she managed to slow down and savour the taste. No other onigiri could ever compare to this, she realized. That was how much it had meant to her.

The white form of Kyoto Tower quivered in the water, warped and blurred by the blue sky around it. Crying wouldn't change anything, thought Shiori. She could never go back to that day. She dabbed at her eyes with a white handkerchief and set about fixing her makeup.

Just then, Nagare and Koishi reappeared, as if this was the cue they'd been waiting for.

'How was it?' asked Nagare.

'Oh, it was wonderful. Like I said, my memories are quite hazy, but I'm pretty sure that was the onigiri he made me.'

'That's good to hear.'

'Your oido must be all cold and sore from that rock,' said Koishi.

Shiori's eyes widened. 'My . . . oido?'

'Kyoto speak for your rear end,' explained Nagare with a grin.

'Oh,' said Shiori, getting to her feet. 'I had no idea. Kyoto dialect is so charming.'

Nagare led the way again. Shiori and Koishi followed a short distance behind, walking side by side at an easy pace.

'Was it really the same?' asked Koishi in a low voice.

'To be honest,' murmured Shiori, 'I don't remember it all that well. So if I tell myself it was the same, then that's how it feels – but if someone were to tell me otherwise, I'd probably believe them, too.'

'I guess it's the act of eating it that matters,' said Koishi. 'So you can make your decision.'

'Exactly. It's time I made my mind up once and for all.'

'I know just how you feel. You need something to stop yourself going in circles.'

Shiori nodded silently in response.

'Dad made a test batch as soon as he got back from Murakami. I tried one myself, and honestly, I can't remember the last time I enjoyed an onigiri so much.'

'He went to Murakami?' asked Shiori.

'Yes. Stayed a couple of nights, too. I wish I could have joined him.'

'I feel bad sending him all that way . . . though I guess it makes sense. I mean, how else was he going to recreate it?' Shiori glanced back at the pond.

'I went to Bettei Haguroan, too,' said Nagare without turning around.

'You . . . did?'

'Wasn't able to meet Yasuhiko, sadly.'

Shiori said nothing.

'Still, your memory might be a little vague, but I'm fairly certain the onigiri you just ate is near enough identical to the one he made for you that day.' Nagare stopped and faced her. 'Can I tell you what I learned at the restaurant?'

Shiori visibly braced herself. 'Okay.'

'They've been in business for over a hundred years,' said Nagare, walking alongside her now. 'It's a grand old ryotei, on par with the finest in Kyoto.'

'I've only eaten there once,' said Shiori, 'and that was just for a bento, not the real deal. Yasuhiko didn't talk about it much, either. But I knew it was a prestigious sort of place.'

'There's a big Tanabata festival in Murakami, isn't there? I was told it's the busiest day of the year for the restaurant. Regulars turn up from all over the city, and some from even further afield. The okami who runs the place told me they offer a special menu that day. And when I asked, she was kind enough to serve me it.'

'Yasuhiko told me the same thing. He said it was a pretty demanding workplace at the best of times, but Tanabata was something else.'

'Here's the meal in question,' said Nagare, producing a photograph from the pocket of his samue and showing it to her.

'Wow,' murmured Shiori. The photo showed an array of extravagant-looking dishes on a table. 'I don't even know what half of those are . . .'

'It was quiet when I visited, so the okami served me herself. She told me all sorts while I ate. The festival menu turned out to be entirely salmon-based, but the fish was of such high quality and so inventively prepared that I enjoyed every mouthful.'

As Nagare spoke, Shiori's grip on the photo tightened.

'Apparently, the whole time they've been in business, a customer has only cancelled on festival day once – and that was four years ago. There were five portions left over, and the head chef divided them up among the younger cooks. They set about packing them into bento boxes – except Yasuhiko, who started making onigiri instead. When the okami asked why, he grinned at her and said he was planning a marriage proposal. She remembered all this like it was yesterday, which is why I was able to recreate the onigiri so closely.'

'So the filling was salmon?'

'Yes. Among the many dishes on the menu, the most prized was the sake no sakabitashi – sake-marinated salmon. A delicacy that takes a huge amount of time and effort to prepare.' Nagare showed her another photo.

'It looks amazing,' said Shiori.

'That wasn't all, though. Yasuhiko had the idea of mixing chopped pieces of soy-marinated salmon belly into the filling. The okami remembers being impressed by that. Said it must have given it an even richer flavour.'

'That sounds just like Yasuhiko. He always wanted to add some little flourish of his own.'

Nagare smiled warmly. 'The okami told me that they use Koshihikari rice from Iwafune at the restaurant. Even told me the exact supplier they use, so I was able to get hold of some. The nori's from the Sea of Japan, while the filling, as I've just explained, is identical. All told, I believe it's the exact onigiri you ate that day. Of course, it might not have tasted quite the same to you. I put my heart into making them, but there's no way I could rival what Yasuhiko was feeling as he worked the rice. Not even a master chef could. When you're making onigiri, technique only gets you so far. It's the emotion you put in that really counts.'

'Right. I guess that's why he chose to make them.'

'Nowadays those "onigirazu" things are all the rage – more like a rice sandwich than a rice ball, and you don't even shape them by hand. That's no way to make a meal. Onigiri taste good because they're moulded with feeling. You think of the person who's going to eat it, transfer all that emotion to the palms of your hands, and press the rice together lovingly. That, to me, is what an onigiri is all about.'

'I can't thank you enough,' said Shiori, smiling radiantly. 'I think I've finally understood what was going through Yasuhiko's head that day. I feel like I can move on at last.'

'Well, that's good to hear,' replied Nagare.

With Koishi following in silence, they passed through the garden's gate and back into the street.

'Oh,' said Shiori, reaching into her bag for her wallet, 'I almost forgot to pay.'

'We don't have a fixed fee. Just send us whatever feels right,' explained Koishi, passing her a slip of paper with their details.

'Alright. I'll see to it as soon as I get back to Tokyo.'

'There's no rush,' said Nagare, pausing as they arrived in front of the Kamogawa Diner. 'Whenever you have time.'

'I really appreciate everything you've done for me.'

With these words, Shiori set off west along the street.

'Ms Yukimura!' Koishi called. When Shiori turned, she said in a quieter voice: 'I hope you find happiness.'

'Thank you. I hope so too.' With a deep bow, Shiori turned and went on walking, her beige scarf trailing behind her in the wind.

'No sign of Drowsy today,' said Nagare, glancing around the front of the restaurant. 'Must be off on an expedition.'

'I bet he's over at Hiroshi's place. He's been heading there lots recently.'

'Probably being fed lots of tasty fish.'

'You're always so tough on him, but deep down, you really worry about that cat, don't you, Dad?'

'Who said I was worried about him? If anything, this place looks neater without him.'

They stepped inside, and Koishi slid the door closed behind them.

'Onigiri for dinner, then?' she asked, glancing playfully at him.

'Bit chilly for that. How about salmon hotpot? The okami at that restaurant told me about one the chefs make for each other at the end of the night.'

'Sounds perfect. We've still got plenty of that Hakkaisan sake you brought back for me, too.'

'Why don't you go pick up Drowsy? You could invite Hiroshi round for dinner while you're at it.'

'You know what? I think I might.'

'Your mother loved her salmon, didn't she?' said Nagare, turning towards the family altar.

'Shame she can't join us for some of this fancy stuff.'

'Well,' said Nagare, who had begun sharpening a knife, 'she'd want us to enjoy it while we can.'

'Hey, Dad.'

Nagare's hands stopped. 'What?'

'How did Yasuhiko die?'

'Ah.' He went on sharpening. 'You picked up on that, then. It was two years back. Scooter accident. He was on his way back from stocking up on ingredients at the market.'

'I had a feeling. Shiori must have known too, right?'

'Of course. There's no way news like that wouldn't have reached her.'

'And yet she still waited four years,' said Koishi as she rinsed out a cooking pot.

'I guess that's how deep her feelings ran.'

'But . . . it's not like she promised to wait. Anyway, what's the point in waiting for someone who's already dead?'

'Koishi. Promises aren't really made with words. They're made in here.' He tapped his chest. 'And once you've made them, they're not easily broken. She kept hers, and we should admire her for it.'

'I guess. But still . . .'

'I'm keeping a promise of my own, you know.'

'Hear that, Mum? Says he's keeping his promise. Who knows how long that'll last, eh?'

Koishi was addressing the photograph on the family altar. For just a moment, Kikuko seemed to smile gently back.

Chapter 3:
Shogayaki

1

Toshio Harasawa stepped off the Keihan line at Shichijo station and took the elevator up to ground level. From Sakai, just south of Osaka, it had taken him two changes of train to get here. Now he was standing practically on the banks of the Kamogawa. He remembered being told that, although the restaurant he was visiting shared that name, it had no connection to the river.

He was wearing a beige jacket and grey slacks. It was a casual enough outfit, but his movement felt oddly constricted. That probably had something to do with the weight he'd gained since taking semi-retirement.

Puffing slightly as he ambled west along Shichijo-dori, Toshio reflected on his newfound life of leisure. He was still chairman, of course, but only in name. When he did venture into the office, there was very little to keep him there, and he was usually gone in under an hour. He spent the rest of his time roaming Sakai or Namba, ducking into whatever restaurant caught his eye for an unhurried lunch and an afternoon tipple. With a routine like that, it was no wonder he was getting a little plump. Even on this chilly day in late autumn, a short walk was enough to leave his forehead damp with sweat.

After crossing Kawaramachi-dori, he turned north at the third small street, then west at the second, glancing at his notes and map as he walked, until he arrived at what appeared to be his destination.

There was no sign, no noren curtain outside, nothing that said 'restaurant'. He'd been expecting this, but it still made him hesitate. He took two deep breaths to steel himself, then slid the door open.

'Hello there,' came the cheerful voice of a young woman in a black sommelier apron.

Toshio's relief showed in his face. 'Is this the Kamogawa Diner?'

'It is,' the woman replied, but said nothing further. Feeling a new twinge of doubt, Toshio ventured his next question.

'I heard you offer a food detective service?'

'Ah. Yes, you're talking to the right person.' The woman bowed. 'Koishi Kamogawa, head of the Kamogawa Detective Agency.'

'Toshio Harasawa. From Sakai.' He produced a business card from his jacket and offered it to her.

'Sakai, did you say?' said a man who had emerged from the kitchen. 'Thanks for making the trip. Nagare Kamogawa – I run the restaurant.' He doffed his cap and bowed.

'And I'm in charge of the agency,' explained Koishi, 'though it's Dad here who does most of the actual investigating.'

'Well, it's a pleasure to meet you both.' Toshio handed one of his cards to Nagare, who put on his glasses, studied the card and then glanced up.

'*Chairman – Harasawa Precision Engineering Ltd.* Sounds impressive.'

'It's a fancy name for what's really just a small workshop. We make machine parts.'

Nagare replaced his cap. 'Hungry? If you don't mind having the set menu, I can bring something out right away.'

'I hate to impose on you like this, but that does sound good.'

'Just a moment.' Nagare disappeared into the kitchen.

'Please,' said Koishi, pulling out a red folding chair from one of the tables, 'take a seat.'

'Much obliged.' Perching on the chair, Toshio glanced around the restaurant.

'So, tell me. How did you hear about us?' asked Koishi.

'There's a bar I go to in Kita-Shinchi. The lady who runs

it told me about this place. Said you'd be able to recreate a dish from my past.'

Koishi paused in the middle of pouring his tea. 'Kita-Shinchi in Osaka? Isn't that a pretty high-end area?'

'Sure. Osaka's version of Gion, if you like. Very different place to Sakai, in any case,' Toshio said with a faint grin.

'What's Sakai like, then? I've never been.'

'Well, let's see . . . there are plenty of factories, trains running right through the city . . . oh, and it's close to the sea, so the seafood's pretty special,' explained Toshio somewhat absent-mindedly.

'I remember seeing something on TV about a tempura place that opens just before midnight and stays open until dawn. That's in Sakai, right?'

'You're well informed! Yes, I've been there a few times myself. That place stays busy all night long.'

'Tempura in the middle of the night, eh? People in Sakai must have strong stomachs.'

'That's the funny thing. You don't get that greasy feeling afterwards. Maybe because the ingredients are so fresh.'

'Really? You're making me want to go.'

The two went on chatting until Nagare emerged from the kitchen with a large round tray.

'Here we go,' he said, setting the entire tray down in front of Toshio. It was filled with small dishes.

Toshio leaned back, his eyes widening in disbelief. 'This is all . . . for me?'

'I know it looks like a lot,' said Koishi, 'but the portions are actually quite small. Now, can I get you something to drink?'

'I do like a tipple,' said Toshio, before giving a wry chuckle. 'But it has a habit of getting me into trouble.'

'You can always stick with tea,' Koishi suggested with a smile.

Toshio grinned back at her. 'Then again, with a spread like this, it'd be rude not to . . .'

'Sake, then?' she asked.

'Please. Something light would be good.'

'Got it.'

As Koishi retreated to the kitchen, Nagare came and stood at Toshio's side. 'Shall I go over the menu?'

Toshio sat up in his seat. 'Please.'

'So, there are nine dishes in total. The Raku plate in the top left is grilled autumn aubergine with a red-and-white miso glaze. On the Kutani plate are some prawns wrapped in yuba – tofu skin, that is – and deep-fried. Try dipping them in the yuzu salt. In the wicker basket on the right is my battered venison, fried Tatsuta-style – that's already seasoned, so you can eat it as it is. Below that, on the blue-and-white porcelain, is the grilled atsu-age tofu with bonito flakes. On the square white dish in the middle is the deep-fried fugu with a ponzu sauce. To the left of that, in the Oribe bowl, is kombu-cured sea bream sashimi – nice with a dab of the yuzu and chilli paste and a bit of soy sauce. The glass bowl beneath that is crab meat: add a dash of the soy sauce vinegar and wrap it with the thinly sliced cucumber. In the middle of that bottom row, on the red-patterned dish, is simmered Yoro pork – best eaten with a good dollop of mustard. And finally, on the Shigaraki plate at the end, you have the matsutake mushroom – deep-fried Western-style, with a Worcestershire sauce.'

Koishi reappeared with a red-lacquered sake flask and cup, which she set beside the tray. 'This is Hakkaisan. Hope it's to your liking!'

'Thank you. I'm no sake expert, if I'm honest,' said Toshio, reaching for the lipped flask and filling the large cup to the brim.

'It being autumn, today's rice is steamed with saury,' added Nagare. 'Just let me know when you're ready for it.'

'And let me know if that sake's running low,' Koishi chimed in. 'Enjoy!'

The pair disappeared back into the kitchen. Alone now in the dining area, Toshio allowed his eyes to wander slowly across the neatly arranged dishes. Each was beautifully presented – and, even more importantly, looked utterly delectable. Toshio cleared his throat, then reached for his chopsticks.

He was no stranger to fine dining. In Sakai, he frequented

a kappo restaurant, while in Minami – Osaka's southern nightlife district, and just a short train ride away – he was familiar with a dozen or so high-end eateries. The Sakai place was fairly informal, with the feel of a casual izakaya, but the Minami spots were luxury ryotei restaurants, and at least half of them had Michelin stars. And yet Toshio could tell, almost immediately, that the food in front of him was in a class of its own.

The presentation wasn't showy, nor were the dishes attempting some sort of bold statement. They were modest, restrained and exquisite, like a set of finely burnished silverware. They had a sort of dignified purity. Somehow, the word 'trustworthy' came to mind.

First he reached for the sea bream sashimi, which was served on the kombu it had been cured between. He set a tiny dab of the yuzu and chilli paste on one of the slices, dipped it lightly in the soy sauce, and brought it to his lips.

It was a dish he'd eaten countless times before, but he didn't remember it ever having such depth of flavour. Whether it was thinly or thickly sliced, sea bream had a habit of being overwhelmed by the ponzu or soy sauce it was served with. He realized now that he'd never really tasted the fish itself. He couldn't say if the secret lay in the particular catch Nagare had sourced, or the way it had been cured with the kombu. In any case, Toshio finally understood why sea bream was known as the 'king of fish'.

After half a cup of the Hakkaisan, he moved on to the crab meat. As instructed, he seasoned it with the soy sauce vinegar, wrapped some of the meat in a slice of cucumber and slipped it into his mouth. The flavour was sharp, briny and exquisite.

He'd taken his staff on numerous trips to hot-spring resorts in the San'in region, famous for its crab – even timing their visits to coincide with the start of the crab-catching season. Meanwhile, at the restaurants in Minami, crab was often the star of the show in winter. But as pricey as all those meals had been, they couldn't hold a candle to this.

Toshio didn't consider himself a connoisseur, but these two dishes were enough to tell him that Nagare was an exceptionally talented chef. Enjoying a mouthful of sake in between each bite, he emptied the red-lacquered flask in no time.

'Shall I top that up for you?' asked Koishi, emerging from the kitchen right on cue.

'Please.' He handed her the flask.

Just as that bar owner in Kita-Shinchi had told him, the restaurant was a far cry from the bustling sort of place its name suggested. In fact, he felt more at ease here than in most luxury establishments.

Finally, after working his way through the nine dishes with quiet reverence – and polishing off two flasks of sake in the process – Toshio was jolted by a realization. The person he most wanted to share this meal with was not his wife.

'Is it about time for that rice?' asked Nagare, noticing the empty dishes.

'Please.' Toshio smiled at Nagare. 'You know, I can't remember the last time I lingered over a meal like this.'

'That's good to hear. I'll have it ready in a moment.'

Toshio toyed idly with his empty sake cup, savouring the aftertaste of everything he'd eaten and wishing it had never come to an end. Then a small earthen pot was placed in front of him, and a rich aroma rose to his nostrils.

'It's nothing too fancy, but I did get hold of some good saury.' As Nagare loosened the rice with a wooden paddle and began spooning it into a blue-and-white porcelain bowl, the aroma grew even stronger. Toshio gulped in anticipation.

'You've taken out the bones, I see?'

'Most of them – but there might be a few tiny ones left, so take care. If you like, you can add some minced sudachi peel and perilla leaves.' Nagare set the bowl of saury rice down together with the pot.

'I often skip grilled fish because of the hassle of picking out the bones. But this way, I get to just enjoy it.' Toshio took a pinch of the minced sudachi and perilla, scattered it over the rice, and reached for his chopsticks.

'Here's some hojicha, too,' said Nagare, setting down

a teapot. 'If you feel like pouring it over the rice halfway through and turning it into ochazuke, you might want to add some of this matcha salt, too. Either way, enjoy!'

Tucking his tray under one arm, Nagare slipped back through the curtain into the kitchen.

When Nagare had mentioned that the rice was steamed with saury, Toshio had pictured a whole grilled fish on top of a bowl of rice. Instead, the dish in front of him had a surprisingly rustic simplicity. The flesh of the fish had been mixed in so thoroughly that he could almost have been looking at a bowl of plain white rice. And yet once he'd sampled its delicate, refined flavour, he found it impossible to stop.

It was hard to tell exactly how much rice was in the pot, but after two refills, and a third which he turned into ochazuke, only a small mound remained. Patting his bulging stomach, he drained the last of the tea.

'Did that agree with you, then?' asked Nagare, poking his head through the curtain.

'That'd be an understatement,' said Toshio, breaking into a broad smile. 'I haven't had anything this good in years.'

'Glad to hear it. Now, when you're ready, I'll show you to the back.'

'Right. I almost forgot the most important part.'

'There's really no rush,' said Nagare, pouring some more tea into Toshio's cup. 'Take a moment to settle your stomach if you like.'

'Oh no – I don't want to keep your daughter waiting.' Toshio drained the tea and got to his feet.

'This way, then, please.'

He led Toshio down a corridor lined with photographs of food. When Toshio commented on them, Nagare turned and smiled. 'I've always loved cooking. Whenever my wife said she was craving something, I'd insist on making it myself.'

'She doesn't help out at the restaurant, then?'

Nagare's smile grew wistful. 'No. These days she keeps an eye on us from the altar instead.'

'I'm sorry,' said Toshio, bowing deeply. 'I didn't mean to—'

'That's alright. Anyway, Koishi will see you now.' Nagare opened the door at the end of the corridor, then turned and made his way back to the restaurant.

Seeing Toshio hesitate in the doorway, Koishi called out: 'Come in, then!'

Toshio felt like he was back at school, and Koishi was a teacher beckoning him into the staff room.

'Sorry to keep you waiting,' he said as he stepped inside. Koishi, now wearing a smart black trouser suit, was smiling at him from the other side of a low table.

'You can relax, you know. Make yourself comfortable.'

Toshio did his best to loosen up as he settled onto the long sofa. Koishi had him fill out a form, glanced at it, then got right to the point.

'So, Mr Toshio Harasawa, what dish are you looking for?'

Toshio had been expecting a little more small talk, and her abruptness startled him. He sat up, leaned forward and said, 'Pork shogayaki.'

'Shogayaki, eh? One of my favourites. Did you have it at a restaurant?'

'No. Someone made it for me.'

'Someone, eh? Very mysterious. Mind telling me the details?' Koishi opened her notebook and leaned forward attentively.

Toshio let out a sigh. 'I should warn you – it's not a very edifying story.'

Koishi's expression softened. 'Whatever you're comfortable sharing.'

Toshio took a moment to get things straight in his mind, then began to speak. 'I inherited the company from my father, who founded it. Business always went pretty smoothly, and we never had any major hiccups while I was in charge. When I hit sixty, I handed the company over to my son. I'm still chairman on paper, but I'm basically retired. I spend most of my days just sort of . . . enjoying myself.'

Koishi's eyes lit up. 'You get to live it up, and the money still comes rolling in? Sounds like the dream.'

'It's not quite as nice as it sounds,' replied Toshio, his gaze dropping to the table. 'Back when I was slaving away every day, I couldn't wait to retire. But now that I'm free, life has started to feel a little empty. Like the world doesn't need me any more.'

'Really? I'd give anything to live that sort of a life.'

'Take it from me: without work to keep you busy, things get very dull, very quickly.'

'Okay, so you miss work, but what about home? After all those years at the company, your wife must be glad to have you around again.' As Koishi leaned forward again, Toshio shrank back slightly.

'Sayo is five years younger than me, and ours was an arranged marriage. I was twenty-eight and she was twenty-three. A marriage like that has its advantages, but it comes with its fair share of problems, too.' Toshio gave a gruff cough. Koishi slid a cup of chilled tea across the table. 'She's from Matsue. Shy, not much of a people person. The stay-at-home type. She's never been interested in travelling or dining out. She prefers to cook things herself, but it's only ever the same few dishes.' Toshio shook his head as he spoke, as if puzzled even now. 'The truth is, I've never really understood what she enjoys in life.'

'Marriage does sound like a tricky old business. Even if

you get on, it must be hard to enjoy each other's company when you have such different lifestyles.'

'Exactly. I've always loved travelling and eating out, so it used to really bother me. At first she forced herself to come along for my sake, but eventually that became too much for her.' He gave another deep sigh and took a sip of the tea. 'About five years into our marriage, we stopped going on trips together, and only ate out on special occasions. She seemed happier that way. But to me something always felt missing.'

'I can imagine,' murmured Koishi sympathetically.

'It wasn't that I resented it. If that was what made Sayo comfortable, then I wasn't going to complain. In a way, it meant I could live at my own pace.'

Koishi glanced up at him. 'So . . . how does the shogayaki fit into all this?'

'Right. I'll get to the point.' He took another sip of tea and went on. 'Five years ago, I went to a high-school reunion at a hotel in Sakai. They'd been having them every three years, but I'd always been too busy with work to attend. But this time I went – and, well, it turned into something of a fateful encounter.' Toshio's cheeks had flushed red, and he seemed to breathe a little faster.

'A fateful encounter?' asked Koishi, readying her pen with renewed interest.

'I ran into my old sweetheart. It had been over three

decades, but the moment I saw her face, it was like all those years had never passed. I'd aged, of course, but she looked just how I remembered her. She's a beautiful woman.'

'May I ask the name of this beautiful woman?'

'Miyuki Yamato.'

'I'm guessing she made the shogayaki.'

Toshio nodded, a shy boyish grin spreading across his face. 'There were lots of other people at the reunion, so we just had a catch-up, said goodbye, and that was that. But afterwards I couldn't stop thinking about her. So, a month later, I went to visit her. She lives in Mimasaka, near Okayama.'

'Can I just get something straight?'

'Go ahead.'

'Sorry to be so blunt, but – you were, and are, married. Yes? And what about this Miyuki in Mimasaka?'

'She's single. She married not long after high school and moved to Mimasaka, but her husband died young.'

'In other words, you were having an affair.'

Toshio lowered his gaze. 'Yes.'

'And you want us to recreate a meal your mistress made for you. Have I got that right?' A jagged edge had come into Koishi's voice.

'That's right,' answered Toshio in little more than a whisper. Koishi said nothing, her fingers tightening around the pen. 'I know it isn't a very decent thing to ask.'

'. . . But you figured we'd help you regardless,' said Koishi quietly.

'Is there any chance you could see your way to taking this on?'

There was a pause. Then, having regained her composure, Koishi sat up and flipped to a new page in her notebook. 'Alright.'

'I really appreciate it.'

'So, a month after the reunion, you paid Miyuki a visit, and that's when she made you the shogayaki?'

'Not quite. She first cooked it for me a year or so after the reunion.'

'Wait. You carried on with her for a whole *year*?' asked Koishi, the edge coming back into her voice.

'I'm embarrassed to admit it, but for a total of three and a half years, Miyuki and I were . . .' Toshio swallowed the rest of his sentence.

'And your wife never found out?'

'My company has a regular client in Okayama, so I'd head there once a month on business and stop by Mimasaka on the way. Sayo never suspected a thing.'

Koishi grimaced slightly. 'Once a month, huh.'

'I honestly never imagined it'd end up that way. I did feel guilty towards Sayo, but I just couldn't stop myself from wanting to see Miyuki.'

'Does she live alone, then?'

'She runs a little cafe on the banks of the Kajinami River, not far from the town hall. Hibiscus, it's called. A kissaten-type place. She lives upstairs. Hibiscuses are my favourite flower, see. Imagine my surprise when I realized she'd named it after them! Every month I'd meet my client in Okayama, then drop by Hibiscus in the evening. I'd sit there waiting in the cafe until six, when it closed, and then we'd go upstairs and have dinner together. That was our routine. I always sat in a corner seat. You know, keeping a low profile. At first I'd insist on heading back to my hotel in Okayama afterwards, but . . . well, Okayama was quite a drive. Before I knew it I'd begun spending the night.' Toshio's cheeks had turned bright red.

'If she runs a cafe, she must be a whizz in the kitchen,' said Koishi, steering them back onto the topic of food.

'Absolutely. Her kara-age chicken and hamburger steaks are out of this world. Of course, she always claimed they were nothing special, that it was only because she made them every day at the cafe. I usually stick to small portions, but whenever I went to Miyuki's, I'd stuff myself silly. I just couldn't help it.' Toshio sheepishly rubbed his stomach. 'A bit like today, actually.'

'Right,' said Koishi flatly. 'And pork shogayaki was your favourite of the lot.'

A smile had spread across Toshio's flushed face. 'It's a dish I've always loved. Back when Miyuki and I were dating, we used to eat it all the time. That's why she made it to mark us being together for another year.'

'Can you describe it to me?' asked Koishi, homing in on her target.

'Well, as I've aged, I've developed a taste for richer flavours – and this dish was the perfect example. Sayo cooks things very mildly, I think out of consideration for my health, but Miyuki seasoned it just the way I liked it. The pork slices were drenched in this thick brown sauce, a bit like the one you have with yakiniku. Went perfectly with a bowl of white rice.' Toshio gulped as he recalled the taste.

'A thick, yakiniku-style sauce that went well with rice,' said Koishi, making a note. 'Anything else that stood out?'

'It wasn't quite as sweet as yakiniku sauce. More of a soy flavour. Miyuki was always boasting that it was her secret blend.'

'And what cut of pork are we talking about? Loin or belly?'

'Loin, I think. Not as thickly cut as usual – more like the sort of slices you'd use for sukiyaki. She'd fry it with cabbage, onion, spring onion and bean sprouts. That was about it.'

Koishi bent forward, pen racing across her notebook as she took down his every word. 'Right. I think I've just about got the picture. And if you want us to recreate it, I'm guessing that means you and Miyuki have broken up.'

She looked him in the eye. 'Otherwise you'd just ask her to make it for you.'

'Yes. About a year and a half ago, I stopped by Hibiscus as usual, but Miyuki looked like she'd seen a ghost. When she told me what had happened, I was stunned.' Toshio took a final sip of his ice tea and went on. 'See, when we met at that reunion, I told Miyuki my wife had passed away, too. That's how desperate I was for us to hit it off. I never managed to tell her the truth afterwards. It turned out one of her friends had found out that Sayo was still alive.' He let out a long sigh.

'You were lying to both your wife and your mistress at the same time?' blurted Koishi, her voice rising. 'Sorry, but just how deceitful can one man be?'

'I knew I had to tell Miyuki the truth sooner or later – not to mention Sayo,' Toshio went on in a low voice. 'In fact, I was planning on coming clean, divorcing Sayo, and starting a new life with Miyuki.'

'Miyuki must have been devastated.'

'Yes. It wasn't just that Sayo was alive – the real shock was that I'd been lying to her all that time. She was furious. Said she could never forgive me.'

'Well, obviously!' exclaimed Koishi, nostrils flaring in indignation. 'If your wife really had passed away, what you and Miyuki had would be a love story. But she's alive, which means it was just an affair. That's quite a distinction.'

'At the reunion I never imagined things would go that far between us. The lie just sort of slipped out.'

'So, what happened next?'

'She told me she never wanted to see my face again, and kicked me out of the cafe.'

'And that was the last time you saw her?'

Toshio nodded silently in response.

'You said it's been a year and a half. What made you want to eat the shogayaki again all of a sudden?'

He leaned forward earnestly. 'To be honest, I'm having trouble getting over her. I thought if I could just keep eating the shogayaki, it might help break the cycle somehow.'

Koishi gave a puzzled tilt of her head. 'Won't it just make you miss her even more?'

'The other day, I asked Sayo if she could try making shogayaki the way I like it. She replied that I'd have to find her a recipe that matched my preferences. That if she made it her way, she knew I wouldn't like it. I know it's horribly selfish of me, but I just feel like if Sayo could make the same dish at home, I'll finally be able to move on.'

'You really think so? Something tells me it'll just have the opposite effect. You really are trying to have your cake and eat it, aren't you?'

'I can't really argue with that. But I promise I'm not trying to rekindle anything. You can take my word for it.'

'Right,' said Koishi, closing her notebook. 'I guess we'll leave it at that.'

The pair returned to the restaurant. Nagare was busy in the kitchen, but came out to talk to them.

'Get all the details?' he asked Koishi.

'Oh yes,' she replied, shooting Toshio a look. 'The whole story.'

Toshio made a low bow in Nagare's direction. 'I'm counting on your help.'

'We'll do the best we can,' replied Nagare, removing his cap and bowing politely back.

Toshio pulled out a bulging wallet and asked to pay for the meal, but Koishi told him that could wait until his next visit.

'And when will that be?' he asked.

'We'll probably need two weeks or so,' said Nagare, glancing at Koishi and then back at Toshio. 'Will that work?'

'Absolutely. There's no rush, so just let me know and I'll come up from Sakai.'

Toshio slid the door open and stepped outside.

'Drowsy, you're in his way,' said Nagare, extricating the tabby cat from between Toshio's legs.

'This is your cat, then?' said Toshio, bending down and gently rubbing Drowsy's neck.

'He's half pet and half stray, really,' said Koishi, scooping the cat up into her arms. 'A sad old existence, don't you think?'

'Miyuki loved cats too. Even slept with hers at night. But she never once let it into the cafe.'

'Well, no,' interjected Nagare. 'You can't have a cat running around when you're serving food!'

Toshio blinked in surprise. 'That's exactly what she used to say.'

'Seems a little excessive, if you ask me,' said Koishi, holding the cat aloft.

'Well, I'll look forward to hearing from you in two weeks.' Toshio turned to face east down Shomen-dori.

'Kyoto station's the other way,' said Koishi.

'The Keihan line's easier for Sakai. I'll hop on at Shichijo.' Toshio gave a quick bow, then walked slowly off down the street.

'So,' said Nagare as they watched the figure recede into the distance, 'what's he after?'

'Shogayaki.'

'From some famous restaurant?'

'No,' said Koishi bitterly, setting Drowsy back down. 'He wants us to recreate the version his mistress used to cook for him.'

'Koishi, it doesn't matter what the customer's circumstances are, our job is to—'

'To find their food. I know, Dad. I haven't forgotten.' Koishi sounded like she was trying her utmost to persuade herself that this was true.

'And where does this mistress live?'

'Mimasaka, near Okayama. Though who knows if she's still there.'

'Only one way to find out, I suppose. Mimasaka's famous for its three hot springs, you know. How about you tag along and we make a trip of it?'

Koishi's face lit up. 'Definitely. I haven't been to an onsen in ages. My skin could do with a boost.'

2

As Toshio emerged from Shichijo station and into the street, the wind that surged up from the river was cold enough to make him hunch over. At least he'd opted for his thickest jacket. He glanced down to confirm that its buttons were fastened.

Just two weeks ago, the weather had still been mild enough for him to break into a sweat. Now, as he crossed the Shichijo bridge, he had to turn his collar up against the cold. There was no mistaking it – winter was closing in.

Scarlet maple leaves swirled and danced in the wind. Toshio was reminded of the time he and Miyuki had been to see the autumn colours in the Okutsu Valley, and the night they had shared at a riverside ryokan. It was one of his fondest memories.

That evening, when he'd slid open the veranda doors, a single red maple leaf had come sailing in on the breeze and landed in Miyuki's hair. She'd dropped it into her cup of sake, a smile spreading across her flushed cheeks. It felt like only yesterday – and like a lifetime ago.

He was more sure of his way this time, and arrived at the Kamogawa Diner in no time.

'Drowsy, was it?' he said to the cat dozing in a sunny patch in front of the restaurant. 'You poor thing. Stuck outside with winter on the way.'

Koishi pulled up on a bicycle, a tote bag in its basket. It seemed she'd been shopping for ingredients. 'When it snows, we line this basket with the blanket and let him sleep in there. So he can keep warm at least.'

A tender look came over Toshio's face. 'Miyuki used to do that, too.'

Koishi glanced at him wordlessly, then slid open the door. 'Please, come on in.'

Toshio stepped inside, somewhat hesitantly.

'Ah,' Nagare called out warmly, 'good to see you. We've been looking forward to this.'

'Me too.' Toshio removed his jacket and draped it across the back of a chair.

'I think you'll enjoy the food.'

At the sight of Nagare's confident grin, Toshio felt a rush of anticipation. Koishi guided him to the same seat as last time.

'I must have put you to quite a bit of trouble.' Toshio produced a digital camera and set it down on the table.

'Not at all. Planning on taking photos?'

'Sayo asked me to. Said they'd serve as a reference.'

'You better cherish her, you know,' said Koishi, giving him a sharp look. 'Or you'll get what's coming to you.'

'Oh, she's like a deity in our house. I worship her every day, I promise.' Toshio pressed his hands together as if to demonstrate.

'Will you be having sake again?' asked Koishi as she wiped down the table.

'No, thanks. I want to give this shogayaki my full attention.'

'Right. If you're not drinking, would you like some rice with it?'

Toshio smiled up at her. 'Please.'

Nagare poked his head through the kitchen curtain. 'I've

already got some cooking. The shogayaki will be ready in just a moment.'

'Looks like Dad was one step ahead,' said Koishi proudly.

Toshio's nose was twitching. 'That smells . . . incredible.'

'Won't be long now. You just sit tight.' Koishi set a Shigaraki teapot and blue-and-white teacup down on the table, then headed back into the kitchen.

Left alone, Toshio glanced idly around the restaurant. It struck him now just how much it resembled Miyuki's cafe. The television and miniature shrine that sat on a shelf hanging from the ceiling, the newspapers and magazines on the counter . . .

When Toshio said he wanted to eat the shogayaki again, he'd meant it. But what he truly wanted to know was how Miyuki was getting on, and where life had taken her. Was she still running Hibiscus? Had she found someone new? He hadn't had the courage to find out for himself, but he couldn't bear not knowing, either. Not that finding out would make any difference at this point.

Since their break-up, Toshio had been surprised to discover a serenity and peace of mind he hadn't known in years. Gone was the constant anxiety of Sayo finding out – and he didn't want it to ever come back.

'Here you are – one shogayaki set,' said Koishi in a playful tone as she set the dishes down.

'Yes, yes . . .' said Toshio, grinning as he took it all in. 'This is just how it was. Even the plates look the same!'

'I was right, then,' said Nagare, arriving at the table. 'Something told me she'd be using Bizen ware. It's just round the corner from Mimasaka, isn't it?'

'There's more of everything, so just let us know if you want seconds,' added Koishi, and the pair retreated back into the kitchen.

In front of Toshio was a thick Bizen plate, heaped with pork and vegetables, a blue-and-white bowl containing a generous mound of white rice, and a lacquered bowl filled with fragrant miso soup, large cubes of tofu suspended just below the surface. There was also a small dish of pickles: what looked like chopped greens, cucumber, turnip and shibazuke.

Toshio used his chopsticks to retrieve a sauce-glazed piece of pork, wrapped it in a piece of cabbage, and set it atop his rice. Then he brought it to his mouth and, as if descending into a dream, closed his eyes.

The pork was marbled with just the right amount of fat, and its rich flavour, combined with that of the sauce, was perfect with the white rice. When Miyuki made it, he'd enjoyed it with a glass of beer or sake. When he asked for seconds of just the pork with some rice on the side, she'd giggle at his childish tastes. The flavours were so similar he could almost hear her laughing now.

Maybe it was just his imagination, but the more he ate, the more his conviction deepened. Nagare must have met Miyuki and learned the recipe from her directly. Miyuki must still be in Mimasaka, running the cafe. A bittersweet emotion swept through him like some last echo of his youth, and a rueful smile appeared on his face.

As he crunched on the pickled cucumber, Toshio recalled the thrill of walking up those stairs to the apartment above the Hibiscus cafe.

But how had Nagare coaxed the recipe out of Miyuki? Had he mentioned Toshio's name and told her he missed her cooking – or had he just gone to the cafe to try the dish himself, and figured out the recipe on his own?

If Nagare *had* spilled the beans, how had she felt? Had she wanted to see him again, or had she just been irritated? Toshio could barely contain the flurry of emotions in his chest.

As he was setting the final slice of pork on top of his rice, Nagare appeared from the kitchen.

'Well, what do you think?'

'It's . . . identical. I can hardly believe it. How on earth did you pull this off?' Toshio was so eager to learn what had become of Miyuki that the words tumbled out of his mouth.

'Before we get to that, can I bring you another helping?'

'Oh, alright. They say people my age should watch their

calories, but . . .' Smiling bashfully, Toshio handed Nagare the empty Bizen plate.

'More rice, too?'

'Half a bowl would be wonderful.'

Midway through his second portion, a vague unease began to creep over Toshio. What if he couldn't resist the urge to see Miyuki again? Even if Sayo managed to recreate this very dish at home, in the end it was only a plate of food. It had taken him a year and a half to fill the aching gap in his heart, and now he'd torn it open again. He remembered Koishi worrying this would only make him miss Miyuki even more. She had been right.

As he set down his chopsticks, Nagare appeared at his side. 'Guess it's about time we told you how we managed this.'

'Some tea,' said Koishi, setting a Mashiko teapot and Karatsu teacup down on the table.

'Mind if I take a seat?' Nagare asked.

'Please do.'

Nagare perched on the folding chair opposite Toshio.

'You went all the way to Mimasaka on my behalf, then?' began Toshio, doing his best to sound calm.

'It was the only option, really.'

'Thanks for going to the trouble,' said Toshio, half rising from his seat to bow.

'Oh, don't worry about it,' interjected Koishi. 'We

stopped by Yunogo Onsen on the way. Made a proper little holiday out of it.'

Nagare shot her a look. 'I thought we were going to spare him that detail.'

Koishi shrugged playfully. 'Did I say too much?'

'I'm fond of Yunogo myself,' said Toshio. 'Wonderful hot springs.'

'Anyway,' Nagare continued, 'we went to the Hibiscus cafe first.'

Toshio leaned forward eagerly. 'Was it still there?'

'Well, yes, but . . .' Nagare trailed off.

'But what?'

'Miyuki Yamato isn't running the place any more. Her sister-in-law Rikako is in charge now, and she's renamed it Sunflower. She knew all about Miyuki, though. It seems they're very close.'

Toshio's shoulders had sagged with disappointment. 'Right . . .'

'The menu hasn't changed much. So we went ahead and ordered the pork shogayaki.'

'Wait. The shogayaki I just ate was being served in the cafe?'

'When Rikako took over, Miyuki passed the recipes on to her,' said Nagare.

'You only ever went there later in the day,' added Koishi.

'So you never saw the lunch menu. It turns out the pork shogayaki was one of the most popular options.'

'Oh. And all this time I thought she was only making it for me. Munching away on the exact same dish all those customers had eaten, convinced it was something special . . .'

'That's what I was worried about,' Nagare said. 'That the version she made for you might have been different from the one at the cafe. So I'm glad to hear you say it tastes identical.'

He looked pleased with himself, but Toshio's face had clouded over.

'You like your flavours nice and strong, don't you?' asked Koishi, smiling slightly. 'It was a bit too intense for me. Without rice I don't think I'd even get through it.'

'Now that you mention it,' said Toshio, 'it has made me quite thirsty.' He reached for his teacup and drained it in one gulp.

'I was surprised when I tried it, too,' said Nagare, gazing at the empty plate. 'Goes wonderfully with rice, but it seems a bit rich for pairing with a drink.'

'I wonder if Sayo will manage it,' said Toshio, tilting his head thoughtfully. 'She takes quite a . . . minimalist approach to seasoning.'

'There's no need to worry. As long as she has this stuff, she'll be able to whip it up.' Nagare set a bottle of brown sauce down on the table.

Toshio picked it up and studied the label. '*Horumon-udon sauce*?'

'Tsuyama, not far from Mimasaka, is famous for its horumon-udon. Udon noodles stir-fried with offal – real comfort food. Of course, the sauce varies depending on the restaurant, but at home people make it with this stuff. It's not bad as condiments go, and versatile too. Miyuki used it to season her shogayaki.'

'*Soy sauce, miso, sugar, mirin, syrup, garlic, ginger, sesame oil, sesame, chilli pepper* . . .' Toshio read from the label, before setting the bottle back down on the table with an oddly detached air. 'Well, that makes sense. If there's ginger in the sauce too, no wonder the flavour's so strong.'

'We tried stir-frying it with some udon,' Koishi cut in, 'and the results were amazing. Hardly surprising, seeing as that's what it's made for.'

'Unlike this place, that cafe actually gets busy at lunchtime – and when it's just you running the place and you've a bunch of different dishes to prepare, you need your shortcuts. This sauce was one of them.'

Nagare was trying to console him, but the chill in Toshio's chest was only growing more insistent. To Miyuki, had he been little more than another customer? He found himself thinking of all the gifts he'd showered her with. All those handbags and accessories . . .

'We bought a whole case of the stuff, so please take it

home with you. Ought to last you quite a while.' Nagare hefted a heavy-looking paper bag onto the table.

'Much obliged,' said Toshio, rising weakly to his feet and straightening his clothes. He pulled out his wallet and turned to Koishi.

'We'll leave the fee up to you. Just send whatever you feel is fair to this account.' She handed him a slip of paper.

'Alright, then. I'll be sure to recompense you for all this time and effort.'

They said their farewells. As Toshio was stepping out of the door, Koishi said, 'Make Sayo happy, you hear?'

Toshio managed a faint smile. 'Thank you. I will.'

'Autumn's almost over,' she added, brushing a dead leaf from Toshio's jacket.

Nagare picked the dark, wrinkled leaf up and showed it to Toshio, who gazed at it wordlessly. 'Leaves fare no better than flowers in the end, do they? Such a beautiful colour when they're in their prime, and then they end up as these little brown scraps.'

'That's life for you,' said Koishi. 'We all burn out in the end.'

Toshio bowed to them and took his leave.

'I thought you were taking the Keihan line?' said Nagare. 'It's the other way.'

Toshio glanced back at them. 'I think I'll try a different

route home today.' With another slight bow, he continued on his way.

When they'd seen him off, Nagare and Koishi stepped back inside.

'Shogayaki for dinner, then?' said Koishi as she cleared the table.

'We could get the hot plate out and grill it as we eat. How about inviting Hiroshi over? We still have a whole kilo of pork to get through. We'll never finish it on our own.'

'I knew you'd say that. I've already asked him to join us.'

'Well, well! Someone's quick on the draw.' Nagare stepped into the kitchen, rolled up his sleeves and began washing a pot.

'Wait, Dad! You forgot to tell Mr Harasawa the most important part!'

Nagare switched off the tap. 'Steady now. No need to shout at me.'

'Remember what Rikako said? When Miyuki made the shogayaki for Mr Harasawa, the seasoning *wasn't* exactly the same as the one she used in the cafe. She cut back on that udon sauce and added soy sauce and sake. It was her little way of making it special for him!'

'Did she really say that?' said Nagare, turning the tap back on. 'My memory must be getting worse.'

'Wait.' She leaned over and gave him a searching look. 'You left that part out on purpose, didn't you?'

Nagare went on scrubbing away in silence.

Koishi went over to the photo of Kikuko on the family altar. She pressed her hands together in prayer, then murmured, 'I guess this way, he and Sayo might still stand a chance after all.'

Nagare stopped washing the pot, glanced over at her and nodded.

Chapter 4: Hiyashi-Chuka

1

A gleaming black Alphard was gliding west down Shomen-dori.

'Should be around here somewhere,' said Michio Shirai, the white-gloved driver, as he glanced up and down the street. But all he could see were austere shopfronts advertising Buddhist altars, rosaries and robes. Given that Higashi Honganji temple was just around the corner, that was only natural.

'All a bit depressing, isn't it,' murmured Saki Morishita from the rear of the luxury minivan, stubbing out her cigarette in a portable ashtray. 'Maybe this wasn't such a good idea after all.'

'Well, madam, you've come all this way . . .'

'I mean, I was warned it was a shabby little place, but I didn't expect the whole neighbourhood to look so miserable.'

'Still, it's not every day you get the chance to revisit memories from forty years ago.'

'They're not going to magically turn me back into a little girl, Michio. And if I *was* going to travel back in time, thirty years would be plenty. Back to when I was a student in France.' Saki's eyes had taken on a faraway look.

'Might this be it?' said Michio, smoothly pulling the Alphard over. 'Looks like there used to be a sign. And I think I smell food.'

Saki lowered her window a few centimetres, then leaned forward and patted him on the shoulder. 'Go have a look, would you?'

'Certainly, madam.' He unbuckled his seatbelt and hopped out of the car.

Saki had been intrigued enough by the idea of a food detective agency to make the trip here, but now she was beginning to regret letting her curiosity get the better of her. Even if they managed to find what she was looking for, what would that really change?

'This seems to be the place,' said Michio, removing his hat and opening the rear door.

'Right. Thanks.' With a vaguely reluctant expression, Saki stepped down from the minivan and pulled on a stylish sky-blue jacket. It was late enough in spring for Kyoto's cherry blossoms to have already fallen, and yet the wind still carried a chill.

'I'll find a car park and wait there. Just call me when

you're done.' Michio closed the door after her, his phone already in hand.

'Okay,' Saki replied half-heartedly, gazing up at the two-storey mortar building.

Just then, a young woman in a black apron slid the door open and smiled. 'Hi. Come on in!'

'Thanks.' Saki did as instructed, looking distinctly unimpressed.

'You must be Saki Morishita? Thanks for calling ahead. I'm Koishi Kamogawa, head of the Kamogawa Detective Agency.' She dipped her head politely.

Saki frowned. 'Ah. So you're the food detective?'

'Well, it's my dad who does most of the actual investigating.'

'Koishi,' called a kimono-clad woman sitting at one of the tables, 'can I get some more tea?'

Koishi grabbed a pot from the counter and hurried over to the woman's table. 'Sorry, Tae – didn't realize you needed a top-up.' Saki's eyes widened as she spotted the elegant array of dishes on the table.

A man who looked to be in his fifties stepped out from the kitchen. 'Ms Morishita, is it? I hope you're hungry. If you don't mind leaving the menu up to me, I'll whip something up right away.'

Saki glanced again at the dishes on Tae's table, then nodded. 'Please. If you don't mind.'

'This is my dad, by the way,' said Koishi.

'Nagare Kamogawa,' he said, bowing. 'Anything you're not fond of?'

'Not especially,' replied Saki, 'but I'm not a big eater, so if you could keep the portions small . . . Oh, and I'm a little sensitive to sour flavours.'

'Got it. Just give me a moment.' Nagare ducked back into the kitchen.

'Can I get you a drink?' asked Koishi.

'I'll let you know once I've had a look at the food.'

'Alright, then. Please, have a seat.' Koishi guided her to the table next to Tae's.

The gloominess of the street, together with the restaurant's plain interior, had succeeded in dulling Saki's appetite almost completely – until, that is, she saw the dishes laid out at Tae's table.

'Everyone pulls that face when they walk in here for the first time,' said Tae, setting down her chopsticks.

'Really? And what sort of face would that be?'

'The face of someone wondering whether a place that looks like this could ever serve a decent meal.'

'I'm not the only one, then.'

'But then the food arrives, and their faces light up. Watching that happen to people is one of the joys of coming here.' Tae smiled as she dabbed at her mouth with a hand towel.

'Do you dine here often, then?'

'Oh, two or three times a week.'

Saki glanced around the restaurant. 'I have to say, that kimono you're wearing is wasted on this interior.'

'Well, appearances can be deceiving. And that goes for places, food and people alike.'

Tae took a crisp ten-thousand-yen note from her purse and set it on the table. Koishi bustled over, tucked it into her apron pocket and bowed deeply. 'Thanks, Tae.'

But when it came to food, thought Saki, surely presentation was everything. Especially the dishes you served a meal on. That was why she'd agreed to try the food here in the first place. She glanced again at Tae's table. The lacquered tray, the Imari rice bowl, the Kutani plate, the little Bizen dish – they were all miniature works of art.

'Here we are,' said Nagare, arriving at her side with a circular tray laden with food.

Tae peered at the tray and gave Nagare a look. 'I should probably be asking for portions like that, too.'

Nagare grinned. 'Ah, but you've always got such an appetite on you.'

'I must not be as refined as this lady,' replied Tae, motioning to Saki with her chin.

'Oh, I wouldn't call myself particularly refined,' said Saki, giving Nagare a look of her own.

'Well, let me talk you through the dishes. On the green Oribe plate in the top left is cherry sea bream, dressed with young pepper tree leaves and salted kombu. To the right, on the Shigaraki plate, are some namafu dengaku – grilled wheat-gluten cakes glazed with miso. The pale one uses a yuzu-infused miso; the dark red one is the stronger hatcho variety. In the cut-glass bowl on the far right are some baby scallops dressed in ponzu. I've made the ponzu a little sweeter than usual, so the acidity shouldn't bother you. Below that, in the decorated Karatsu dish, is braised tongue – Omi beef, simmered over two nights, best enjoyed with a dab of mustard. The fish on the yellow Seto plate to the left is sawara mackerel, grilled Kyoto-style in a sweet white miso marinade. Try spicing it up with a pinch of kuro-shichimi. The smaller fish on the far left is sweet-simmered moroko, and then below, in the bamboo basket, you have the tempura. Ostrich fern, momijigasa, baby ayu from Lake Biwa, anago eel from Akashi, and hamaguri clams from Ise. All good with sansho salt or the tentsuyu dipping broth – or you might want to try the sesame sauce. Finally, the rolled omelette is dashimaki tamago. I've seasoned it Tokyo-style – a little on the sweet side. Take your time, and enjoy.'

Saki took in his every word, her eyes sparkling at each additional detail.

'Now I see what you meant,' she said to Tae. 'Anyone's jaw would drop at the sight of such exquisite food in a humble little restaurant like—' She glanced up at Nagare. 'Sorry, I hope I'm not being rude.'

'Not at all. I'm aware the place doesn't exactly look enticing to a first-timer.' Nagare smiled as he tucked the round tray under one arm. 'Anyway, there's nothing very fancy about my cooking.'

'Well?' said Tae, looking pleased with herself. 'Better than you expected, isn't it?'

'Oh yes – you were absolutely right. Excuse me – Koishi, was it? I think I will have that sake, you know.'

Koishi turned to face her. 'What kind would you like?'

'Fushimi sake is on the sweeter side, isn't it?'

'Not necessarily,' interjected Nagare, 'but the profile does tend to be milder. There's an old saying about it being more popular with women than the harder stuff you get in Nada.'

'I'll have some of that, then,' said Saki without looking up from the dishes in front of her. 'Slightly chilled, please.'

'Certainly.' Koishi hurried after her father into the kitchen.

'Well, I've had my fun. I think I'll be on my way,' Tae murmured, more to herself than anyone else.

'That really is an elegant kimono, you know,' observed Saki.

'Thank you. It's really nothing special.'

Saki glanced at the obi tied around Tae's waist. 'Are those ayame irises?'

'Kakitsubata, actually. The type that grows in water.' Tae turned slightly to show her the pattern.

'I see. Very summery. I suppose it's good to keep ahead of the season.'

Tae smiled faintly in response. 'Enjoy the meal.'

'Off already, Tae? We'll be looking forward to next time.'

Koishi saw Tae out of the restaurant. Saki, alone now, picked up her chopsticks and reached straight for the dashimaki tamago. She never told people – it seemed a little childish – but she had a soft spot for simple egg-based dishes. She devoured the omelette in no time.

After savouring its sweet flavour, she reached for the Oribe dish and started on the cherry sea bream. The light briny fragrance, the silky mouthfeel, the pleasant firmness of the flesh . . . A single piece of sashimi, and she was captivated. She was particularly impressed by the effect of the delicately chopped pepper tree leaves; she'd expected them to overpower the fish, but instead their aroma blended with that of the sea bream in a way that felt utterly natural.

'And here's the sake,' said Nagare setting a red cut-glass tumbler of the clear liquid down on the table.

'May I ask what it's called?'

'This is Yanagi, brewed by Tsukino Katsura. Dry, but packed with flavour.'

Saki smiled up at him. 'The food is wonderful.'

'Glad you think so. Please – take your time.' Nagare turned towards the kitchen.

'Sorry, but can I ask something?'

Nagare stopped and turned back. 'And what might that be?'

'What's the difference between ayame and kakitsubata irises?'

'Ah.' Nagare gave a pained smile. 'You're referring to Tae's obi.'

'Yes. I mean, I'm sure you can tell them apart in real life, or in a photo. But from the pattern on an obi?' Saki gave an unconvinced frown.

'She always wears that one at this time of year. Apparently ayame only bloom in dry places, like fields, whereas kakitsubata grow in wetlands. Something like that, anyway. More importantly – that's a beautiful brooch you're wearing.' Nagare's gaze had settled on the small, matte black accessory pinned to her sky-blue jacket.

'Thank you. One of my own designs.'

'Reminds me of finely woven bamboo. My wife loved that sort of pattern.'

'Oh. Did she . . . pass away?'

'A while back. I'm a fully fledged widower these days.'

Once Nagare had retreated into the kitchen, Saki slipped off her jacket, revealing an off-white blouse. She glanced around, but found nothing resembling a coat rack. With a resigned sigh, she draped the jacket over the back of her chair.

As a jewellery designer, she prided herself on her eye for

aesthetic detail, but when it came to traditional Japanese motifs – like those irises – she still had a lot to learn. Still, this frustration did nothing to slow the pace of her chopsticks. Between dabbing the ayu tempura in the small mound of sansho salt and savouring the two kinds of miso on the namafu dengaku wheat-gluten cakes, she emptied the red tumbler of sake in no time.

'Top-up?' asked Koishi, approaching from behind with a silver tray.

'Thank you. The same, please.'

'Right away.'

Judging the right moment at which to offer another drink was an art in itself – and Koishi had judged the moment perfectly. The service here was turning out to be just as impressive as the food.

'Here you go,' said Koishi, swapping the red cut-glass tumbler for a blue one. Even the sake cups were clearly chosen with great care.

The grilled sawara mackerel had a gentle sweetness, and its delicate umami danced across her tongue. Surely there was no fish that paired better with sake, she thought, before turning her attention to the simmered beef tongue. It looked almost like a Western-style stew, but the moment she bit into the tender meat, a distinctly Japanese aroma and flavour spread through her mouth. This, too, paired fantastically with the sake. Next, as a palate cleanser, she tried the baby scallops. They were a perfect match for the ponzu – which, as Nagare had noted, was sweet rather than tart.

'Is everything to your liking, then?' asked Nagare, stepping out from the kitchen.

'Truly. I can't remember the last time I ate so well.'

'You're flattering me. I bet you dine at fancy restaurants all the time.'

'I do, but . . . this is on another level.'

'Well, that's music to this chef's ears. The rice is ready, so just let me know when you'd like me to bring it through.' Nagare hastened for the kitchen again as if embarrassed by her praise.

When she was halfway through her second tumbler of sake, Saki decided to sample the item she'd been most curious about: the sesame dipping sauce. She'd eaten tempura countless times – and at some of Tokyo's finest establishments – but she'd never once seen it paired with a sesame sauce. Somewhat warily, she dipped the fried anago eel into the sauce, then brought it to her lips.

Her eyes widened. She let out a loud gasp.

Nagare rushed out from the kitchen. 'Is everything alright?'

'Sorry,' said Saki, hunching her shoulders apologetically. 'I didn't mean to startle you. It's just so good.'

'Well, that's a relief,' said Nagare, grinning to himself as he slipped back through the kitchen curtain.

The dish was a revelation. Saki had never imagined that a sesame sauce – even one like this, which was more savoury than sweet – would pair so beautifully with tempura. In the end, she dipped every last piece in it.

Nagare poked his head through the curtain. 'Is it about time for the rice course?'

'Please. Just a little will be fine, thank you.'

For all her earlier declaration that she wasn't a big eater, Saki had polished off the food in no time.

'I hope this'll be to your liking,' said Nagare, setting a small bamboo basket down in front of her.

'What . . . is it?'

'You know sakura mochi – sweet rice cakes wrapped in cherry blossom leaves? Well, this is sakura sushi. Bite-sized pieces of sushi wrapped in salted cherry leaves. From left to right: kombu-cured sea bream, vinegared mackerel, grilled eel, steamed prawn and simmered octopus. I went easy on the rice, but just leave anything you can't finish. The cherry leaves can be eaten or removed – it's up to you. The soup is a simple clam broth; you might want to add a sprinkle of the chopped pepper tree leaves.'

Saki savoured the sushi one piece at a time, and was enchanted by the bright, refreshing aroma of the soup. *If only I lived in Kyoto*, she thought. *I'd be a regular at this place in no time.*

'Some tea,' said Nagare, setting a Mashiko teapot and colourful Koimari cup on the table.

'I feel silly for saying I didn't eat much.' Saki blushed as she gazed at the empty bamboo basket.

'I'm just glad you enjoyed it,' replied Nagare as he filled the cup with tea.

'I haven't eaten this much in years. My husband would be astonished.'

'Well, if you ask me, cooking is all about the connection between the chef and the diner. And it looks like we hit it off.'

'We did?'

'Definitely. Without that rapport, even the fanciest food in the world falls flat. Anyway, Koishi's just getting ready in the office. I'll show you through now if you like.'

'Of course. I was so taken by your cooking that I almost forgot why I'm here. Lead the way!'

At the end of a long corridor was an office with a placard that read: *The Kamogawa Detective Agency.* Nagare ushered Saki through the door.

She was greeted by Koishi, now wearing a black trouser suit. 'Please, take a seat.'

Saki perched in the middle of the long sofa.

'Do you mind filling this out, and we can get started?' said Koishi, handing her a form on a clipboard.

'I wasn't expecting paperwork,' said Saki as she began writing down her details. 'This is quite the operation.'

'Tea or coffee?'

'Coffee, please,' said Saki. When she'd finished with the clipboard, she set it down on the low table and gazed absent-mindedly at the books on the shelf until Koishi brought over two cups of coffee.

'Ms Saki Morishita, yes? And you're a jewellery designer? Sounds like a lovely line of work.'

'Thank you. I do all sorts of accessories, actually.'

'Now then,' said Koishi, opening her notebook and getting to the point. 'What dish would you like us to recreate?'

'Hiyashi-chuka.'

'As in, reimen? The chilled noodles you get in the summer?'

'No, not reimen. Hiyashi-chuka.'

'Aren't they the same thing?'

'Not at all. Reimen are the Korean-style cold noodles they serve at yakiniku restaurants, while hiyashi-chuka means chilled noodles served in a sweet-and-sour sauce or broth. They're completely different dishes.' Saki cocked her head doubtfully. 'Are you sure I can trust you with this?'

'My apologies,' replied Koishi with an easy smile. 'Must be a Tokyo distinction. Here in Kyoto we call them both reimen. I mean, the word just means "cold noodles".'

Saki's eyes widened. 'But . . . that must get confusing. What if they serve you the wrong dish?'

'Well, yakiniku joints serve the Korean-style noodles, and everywhere else serves the other type. There isn't much room for mix-ups. Anyway,' Koishi continued calmly. 'Tell me about this hiyashi-chuka. When and where did you have it?'

'I had it as a little girl, in the Fukui countryside,' Saki said in a flat tone. 'We used to spend our summers at my father's family home, where my grandmother would make it for me.'

'May I ask her name?'

'Kaneko Sadaoka.'

'So your father's from Fukui, then,' said Koishi, jotting the name down in her notebook. 'Which part, exactly?'

'The Takahama area. I don't know the exact address. We stopped going after I started middle school.'

Koishi's eyes twinkled with recognition. 'Takahama. With the beach where everyone goes to swim?'

'Yes. It was right behind my grandmother's house. But I was never allowed. My mother was very strict about that.'

Koishi stopped scribbling. 'How come? You had the sea right on your doorstep . . .'

'Well, it'd be dangerous, for one thing. And it looked rather dirty.'

'Really? When I was a kid, my mum took me all the time. I used to spend all day splashing about in the sea.'

'My father married into the Morishita family. They had a house in Kotsubo, on the Shonan coast just south of Tokyo. There was a huge pool in the garden, so I swam there instead. I only visited my grandmother in Takahama rarely, when my father insisted on dragging me along.'

Koishi glanced at the form Saki had filled out. 'And you're still living there now – at your mother's family home in Kotsubo?'

'That's right. I had my own house and residence built on the grounds.'

'The Shonan coast, eh? Must be worlds apart from Takahama.'

'You could say that. The Takahama property was large enough, but the house itself was a rickety old wooden structure – and with only my grandmother to look after it, it wasn't in very good shape. The bathroom was so grimy it made my skin crawl.'

'Still, your grandma knew how to make an amazing hiyashi-chuka.'

'That's the strange part. I don't remember it being that special, but my father keeps insisting it was my favourite.'

'Well, if your father says so . . .'

Saki's mouth twisted into a smile. 'If he says so, yes.'

'Pardon me for asking,' said Koishi, 'but you don't seem particularly keen on eating this dish. So why come to us?'

'For some reason, my father has started craving it. He

completely lost his appetite when my mother died last year – and yet day after day he says he wants a bowl of those noodles. I asked him if it was one of his last wishes – if eating them would help him depart in peace.' Saki chuckled softly. 'And he told me it was.'

Koishi's expression had turned solemn. 'Your grandmother in Takahama – Kaneko. Is she still alive?'

'Oh, she's been dead for years. If she were alive I'd have asked her. Obviously.' Saki snorted dismissively. 'I thought you were a detective!'

'I see,' said Koishi, pressing a hand to her chest as if to contain her irritation. 'And your father doesn't remember what the noodles were like?'

'He has . . . well, dementia. I can't make sense of half the things he says. Asking him would get me nowhere.'

'What about the house in Takahama? Is it still there?'

'I wouldn't know,' Saki replied airily. 'We've fallen out of touch with that side of the family.'

'Right. It's just . . . we're going to need a little more to go on. Is there anything else you remember about the noodles? Even the tiniest details can be helpful.'

'Well, I don't know how it's served in Kyoto, but hiyashi-chuka normally comes with shredded cucumber, shredded omelette and a few strips of ham or roast pork on top.'

'Yes, it's the same here. We just call it reimen instead.'

'But my grandmother's version was a little different. It

had the shredded omelette, but the other toppings were simpler. Chicken, shiitake, things like that.'

'Sounds like you remember it just fine.'

'I'm just repeating what my father told me. I don't recall a thing myself.'

'And how did it taste?'

'I'm telling you, it's all a blur! I can tell you how it looked: drab. As for the taste, all I remember is that it didn't have the sourness that hiyashi-chuka usually has. That part at least must have suited my palate.'

'Anything else you recall?'

'She used to serve this sweet milk with it. Whenever we visited, that was the part I would look forward to: the milk.'

'Sweet milk, eh? Alright.' Koishi snapped her notebook closed. 'I'll make sure Dad leaves no stone unturned.'

Back in the restaurant, Saki bowed politely to Nagare. 'I'm ever so grateful for your assistance. Though I'm afraid my memories turned out to be awfully vague, so you won't have much to go on . . .'

Koishi felt a wave of exasperation at Saki's sudden transformation into a gracious and polite person, and looked on sourly as Nagare bowed deeply in return.

'Whatever it is you're after, I promise to give it everything I've got.'

'Excuse me a moment.' Saki reached into her bag for her phone, tapped at it and raised it to her ear. She was asking her driver to pick her up. When Koishi grimaced openly at the brusqueness with which she did so, Nagare made a stern face and shook his head in warning.

'Ah, yes,' said Saki when she was finished, swapping her phone for a bulging blue purse. 'Let me pay.'

'That can wait until next time,' explained Nagare. 'You'll pay for everything together.'

'Alright. And when will that be?'

'Two weeks from today, if that works?'

'Certainly. I'm in no rush.'

'We'll call you on the number you gave on the form.' As Koishi said these words, a car pulled up outside.

'Well, thank you in advance.' Saki dipped her head respectfully towards Nagare and slid open the door.

Once they'd seen her off, Nagare put a hand on Koishi's shoulder. 'How many times do I have to tell you? No matter how a customer acts, our job is to find their food. You can't go pulling faces at them.'

'But Dad – she's asking us to recreate a dish she doesn't even want to eat.'

'That doesn't matter. I'm sure she has her reasons. She came all this way, didn't she?'

'Well, yeah, but . . .'

'What's the dish?'

'Hiyashi-chuka,' Koishi replied coolly.

'As in, reimen?'

Koishi pouted. 'Not according to her.'

'They're the same dish.'

'That's what I thought. But she insists they're different.'

'Well, never mind that. Is it from a restaurant?'

'Her grandmother used to make it for her. Out in the countryside.'

'Sounds like a tough one.'

'Yeah, Dad. This one might test even you.'

'You'd better give me the whole story.'

They sat down opposite each other at one of the tables, and Koishi opened her notebook.

2

Spring was edging into summer. Saki knew it the moment she stepped down from the minivan and felt a warm breeze on her cheeks. She was fuzzy-headed from staying up late the night before to work on a design, and the almost-humid air wasn't helping.

'I don't remember seeing *you* here last time,' she said, bending down to pet the tabby cat that had apparently taken up residence in front of the Kamogawa Diner.

'Hello again,' said Koishi, stepping out to greet her. 'Are you a cat person, then?'

'Yes,' Saki replied. 'Mainly because they don't yap away at you like dogs do.'

'I don't know. Some cats can be pretty vocal,' countered Koishi.

'Yes, but in a friendly sort of way. That's what I like.' Saki rubbed Drowsy gently on his chin, then got to her feet.

'Come on in,' said Nagare from the doorway.

'Well, how did it go?' asked Saki nonchalantly as soon as she was inside.

'I believe we found what you're looking for.'

'Oh, good,' Saki replied in the same flat tone.

'That's another lovely brooch,' said Nagare, gesturing at the accessory pinned to her olive-green jacket.

'Thank you. Again, one of my designs.' Saki raised her head proudly. 'This one's been acquired by an art museum in New York, actually.'

'Funny,' said Koishi, leaning in for a closer look. 'It looks sort of familiar.'

'I shouldn't think so. It's an original design.'

'Right. Sorry.' Koishi still seemed doubtful, but caught Nagare's stern gaze.

'Apologies,' he said, 'my daughter has a habit of speaking out of turn. Now, we'll just get everything set up.' Nagare set a hand on Koishi's shoulder and guided her into the kitchen.

Two weeks had passed, and Saki's feelings were unchanged. She'd come here on a whim in the first place, and was hardly expecting an epiphany. In fact, she was beginning to wonder what the point of all this could possibly be.

'Fine with just tea today?' asked Koishi, emerging from the kitchen with a blue-and-white Tobe teapot and yellow-glazed Seto teacup. 'Or can I get you a drink?'

A faint smile tugged at Saki's mouth. 'I'm tempted, but yes, I'll stick to tea.'

'Ready?' asked Nagare, who had arrived behind Saki with a silver tray.

She turned around. For the briefest of instants, she could have sworn it was her grandmother standing there with the tray.

'These are the noodles your grandmother, Kaneko Sadaoka, used to make you.'

Saki's eyes went straight to the shallow bowl on the tray.

'Grandma . . .' she murmured. The word had slipped unbidden from her lips.

'Thank you for coming all this way, Saki. It's been so long! My, how you've grown . . .'

Saki was sitting in front of a soup bowl decorated with

red flowers. In it was a large portion of her grandmother's hiyashi-chuka.

'Sorry not to have come sooner, Grandma.'

'It's alright, dear. Don't trouble yourself about that – just eat. I made your favourite noodles.'

Kaneko ladled a generous amount of the chilled broth over the noodles. Saki pressed her palms together, said itadakimasu, and got started.

'Don't eat too fast,' her grandmother said tenderly, smiling down at her. 'They'll get stuck in your throat!'

'Mm-hm . . . Grandma, it's so tasty.'

'Nothing makes me happier than hearing you say that, Saki.'

'Grandma, can I have more egg?'

'Of course, dear. I knew you'd ask. I made extra since you like it so much.' Kaneko happily piled more of the shredded omelette onto the noodles.

'Thanks, Grandma. I love it!'

'It's very sweet of you to say that. And I love you.'

Saki worked her way through the noodles in silence.

The boiled chicken had a pleasant saltiness. The shredded omelette was soft and fluffy, the shiitake had been sweet-simmered, and it was all topped with flakes of nori. For all that her grandmother had called it hiyashi-chuka, it had almost none of the tangy sourness associated with that dish. Instead, it was the gentle flavour of dashi stock that prevailed. It was almost like eating a chilled bowl of ochazuke. Saki's chopsticks kept moving.

'Well? Did we get it right?'

Peering down at her was not Kaneko, but Nagare.

'To be honest, I'm not really sure. But . . .'

'But?'

'I didn't think it would make me so nostalgic.'

'Well, I'm glad to hear it did.'

'How did you . . . manage this?' asked Saki. Her eyes had misted over slightly.

'We'll get to that in a moment. First – this.' Nagare set a glass of white liquid in front of her. 'The milk you loved so much.'

A smile of childlike delight spread across Saki's face. 'Oh! Yes, this is it.'

'I'd never heard of this stuff. There are some very curious beverages in the world.'

'Now, this *really* takes me back. Do they sell it in Takahama, then?'

'All will be revealed when you've finished.' Nagare glanced at the half-eaten noodles in the bowl. 'I gave you quite a big serving, so please don't force yourself.'

Saki straightened up in her chair. 'I won't.'

'Though it's mainly toppings, really – there aren't that many noodles. Anyway, take your time.'

Nagare returned to the kitchen, and Saki raised her chopsticks once more. Between nibbling on the toppings and slurping the noodles, she made sure to take small sips of the sweet milk. As she repeated the cycle, she began to hear what sounded like the ocean in her head. The soft crash of the waves, their steady ebb and flow. Lulled by the soothing rhythm, Saki dreamily closed her eyes.

'It's just . . . so good . . .' she murmured.

Saki twined the noodles around the fluffy egg, soaked them in the broth, and slipped them into her mouth. She found herself genuinely wondering if anything else in the world could ever taste this good. It bore little resemblance to the hiyashi-chuka she'd eaten anywhere else. There was a very faint acidity, but nothing you could call sourness. The broth – chicken, probably – was light in flavour, but had the salty richness of shio ramen. It was a curious dish indeed. More puzzling than anything was how unbearably nostalgic it was making her feel. In the end, Saki drained every last drop of broth from the bowl.

'How was that, then?' asked Nagare.

Saki raised herself up from her seat and bowed. 'You've given me the pleasure of eating something truly delicious today. I can't thank you enough.'

'It's Grandma Kaneko you should be thanking. She

dreamed up a sensational dish.' Nagare glanced at the empty bowl, then back at Saki. 'Mind if I sit?'

Saki leaned forward. 'Please. I want to hear the whole story.'

'Koishi,' said Nagare, glancing towards the kitchen, 'fetch me that folder, would you? And some tea. Hojicha would be best.'

'You went all the way to Takahama, then?' Saki began.

'Naturally. But when I got there, things took an unexpected turn.' Nagare took the folder from Koishi and opened it on the table.

'Ah, yes,' said Saki, squinting at a photo of an old-fashioned two-storey building. 'That's the house. You could stroll right down to the beach from the back garden.'

'It's been empty for seven years, but it's actually in pretty good shape. Someone could move in tomorrow without a problem . . .' Nagare cleared his throat. 'But I'm getting ahead of myself. It's quite a long story, see.'

'I'm all ears,' Saki said, reaching for her teacup.

'Do you remember the ryokan that was just behind the house?'

'Hmm. Now that you mention it . . .'

'The Masaki Ryokan, it's called. A relaxed little place – more like a family-run guesthouse, in fact. I stayed there and spoke to the owner, Mr Masaki. He knew Kaneko well.'

Nagare set down a photo of Mr Masaki, standing by the entrance to a weathered old building.

'I see,' said Saki, her face betraying no reaction whatsoever.

'Tell me, have you ever heard the story of how your parents first met?'

'I was told they didn't marry out of love, but I've never heard the details. Why do you ask?'

'Your mother's father, Uichi, loved marine sports and was always out in his yacht. You knew that much, yes?'

'Yes.'

'Once, he took your mother, Hamae, on a cruise down to Amami Oshima, and they got into an accident.'

Saki's eyes widened. 'Really? No one ever told me that.'

'See, Amami Oshima is paradise for marine sports enthusiasts,' said Nagare, unfolding a map. It showed the island of Amami Oshima, some two hundred miles south of the Japanese mainland.

A dubious expression had come over Saki's face. 'Neither my grandfather nor my mother ever mentioned going there.'

'Probably didn't want to bring it up. It may have been quite a painful memory for your grandfather.'

'What exactly happened?'

'He made a steering error, and they collided with a fishing boat. They were both thrown into the sea. Hamae was still a little girl, and almost drowned. It was your father,

Shigeru, who saved her.' Nagare smiled warmly at Saki. 'He was ten years old at the time.'

'My . . . father?'

'That's right. The boat they collided with was captained by his own father, Katsushige, and he happened to be aboard. Katsushige and the crew were so busy trying to save their own vessel that they didn't even notice Hamae, while Uichi had also lost sight of her in the chaos. Shigeru spotted her, and dived in to save her.'

Saki looked shellshocked. 'That . . . really happened?'

'Hamae had breathed in a lot of seawater. After the rescue, she hovered between life and death for five whole days.'

'And that's how my parents met?'

'Exactly.'

Saki gave him a puzzled look. 'But how did that lead to them getting married?'

'Out of gratitude, Uichi began taking Hamae to Amami every year for the summer holidays. And because she and Shigeru were close in age, they grew very close. Almost like brother and sister.'

'They *have* always acted a bit like siblings,' said Saki, her gaze softening slightly. 'The quiet older brother and the mischievous little sister.'

'But it seems Uichi and Katsushige never really managed to get along.'

'Come to think of it, all I've ever been told about my paternal grandfather is that he died young.'

'It makes a sort of sense. Uichi was heir to the Morishita family, a former zaibatsu conglomerate. Katsushige was a humble fisherman. Their circumstances couldn't have been more different. And besides . . .' Nagare seemed to hesitate.

Saki leaned in closer. 'Besides?'

'As I said, Uichi was only visiting Amami to show how grateful he was for his daughter's rescue. But Katsushige began to think he was making advances on Kaneko.'

A quiet sigh escaped Saki's lips.

'It was true that Kaneko, for her part, had begun to feel quite fond of Uichi, though not in the way her husband suspected. But for the headstrong Katsushige, even that was unforgivable. His drinking can't have helped. In the end, he threw her and Shigeru out of the house.' Nagare was relaying the story exactly as he'd heard it from Mr Masaki.

'And that's how they ended up in Takahama?'

'Believing he had separated a wife from her husband, and a son from his father, Uichi offered Kaneko his villa in Takahama. He charged her no rent and asked only that she and Shigeru look after the house. This was about three years after the accident.'

'But . . . Amami to Takahama is a huge distance. If they were going to move all that way, he might as well have put them up in Kotsubo.'

'His wife – your other grandmother, Sadako – was in poor health. I assume he didn't want to worry her.'

'Is that so? I was too young when she passed away to remember much about her,' said Saki in a low, sad voice.

'Twenty years after the accident, Uichi asked Shigeru to marry into the family. That may have been motivated by his affection for Kaneko, but more than anything it was because Hamae looked up to Shigeru like an older brother.'

'More tea?' Koishi broke in.

'Please,' said Saki, sliding her empty teacup forward.

'Both Kaneko and Shigeru agonized over the decision. But in the end, Shigeru married Hamae and took on the Morishita name. As for whether it was the right choice – well, it seems that was a question that occupied Kaneko until her dying day.'

'Why's that?'

'At Hamae and Shigeru's wedding, she was stunned by the gulf between the two families. She'd known about it beforehand, of course, but seeing it with her own eyes was still a shock. She was so worried about tarnishing the Morishita name that she began keeping her distance from Uichi. That must have torn her up inside. Her daughter-in-law even had a baby, whom she was desperate to see, but still she restrained herself. Of course, when you *did* visit, she was over the moon.'

As she listened, Saki was remembering Kaneko's gentle smile.

'I wonder why they couldn't just get along,' Koishi interrupted. 'Is family status really that important?'

'Now that I think about it,' said Saki, letting her gaze wander up to the ceiling, 'Takahama was the only place where my father ever seemed to fully relax.'

'I guess to him it was home, even if Amami was his birthplace,' observed Koishi, reaching for the photo of the Takahama house. 'Kaneko seems to have really doted on him there.'

Nagare, meanwhile, was pointing at Saki's bag. 'Same colour as your jacket, I see.'

Saki hugged the olive-green bag to her chest. 'It's one of my favourite tones.'

'You know, the painter Isson Tanaka used that colour a lot. And as it happens, he was based in Amami Oshima.'

She looked right at him, startled.

'That sky-blue jacket you wore last time was another of his favourite colours. They're the colours of the island.'

'I . . . had no idea.' Saki traced a finger along the sleeve of the olive-green jacket.

'Now, about these noodles. They're actually Kaneko's version of keihan, an Amami specialty. Mr Masaki told me he'd been treated to it a number of times. I believe she devised it especially for you, given your low tolerance for sour flavours.'

'Oh, yes,' said Saki, her voice brightening. 'As a child, I couldn't stand them.'

'You cook the noodles, add the same toppings as with keihan – boiled chicken, sweet-simmered shiitake and shredded omelette – and pour chilled chicken broth over the lot. It's a clever idea – and perfect for summer, when hotter dishes lose their appeal. Even after moving far from the island where she grew up, Kaneko still carried its flavours deep inside her. As for that sweet milk, it's another Amami specialty.'

At a signal from Nagare, Koishi set a carton of milk in front of Saki.

'*Hanada no Miki*?' read Saki. 'Can't say I recognize it.'

The carton was decorated with a red sun and blue waves.

'Miki is a traditional fermented drink enjoyed in Amami and Okinawa. People used to make it at home, but these days there are dedicated manufacturers. It's basically rice, sugar, sweet potato and water. Very sweet when it's fresh, but as it ferments it turns a little sour – which is why children were usually given it right after it was made. What you sipped on with your noodles was, of course, Kaneko's homemade version – freshly prepared.'

'I had no idea I had any sort of connection to Amami,' murmured Saki pensively, her eyes lingering on the label.

'Oh, you have a connection alright,' said Nagare, looking her right in the eyes. 'In fact, I'd go as far as saying that Amami blood is still pulsing through your veins.'

Saki gave a wry smile. 'This all seems a little far-fetched.'

'Tell me. Are you familiar with Oshima Tsumugi silk?'

'I've heard of it, yes. I'm not really a kimono person, so I'm a little hazy on the details, but it's expensive stuff, isn't it?'

'It's expensive, alright,' Nagare explained. 'And it originates from Amami Oshima. My father had a haori made from it. He used to boast that it was a family treasure – though to me it always seemed a little too fancy for our household.'

Koishi produced the silk haori in question and pulled it on over her shirt by way of demonstration.

'The hallmark of Oshima Tsumugi is how all the tiny dots are connected,' said Nagare, examining the haori up close.

Saki was peering at the haori in alarm. 'But . . . that pattern . . .'

'You noticed, then?' Nagare pointed at the brooch pinned to Saki's jacket. 'It's a perfect match.'

'Wow,' said Koishi, glancing at the haori's sleeve and then the brooch. 'It really is.'

Saki shook her head firmly. 'If you're implying I stole that design, I did nothing of the sort . . .'

'Of course not. No one's saying you stole anything. This

is what I meant when I said you have Amami blood in your veins. You designed this brooch without knowing a thing about Oshima Tsumugi, and yet it happens to feature one of its classic patterns – the linked square motif. One brooch might just have been a coincidence, but the accessory you wore last time looked strikingly similar to' – Nagare opened a catalogue – 'this.'

Saki inhaled sharply.

'Another signature Oshima motif,' said Nagare. 'The wickerwork pattern.'

'Incredible . . .' murmured Koishi, her eyes widening as she leaned in to look.

Saki gave a resigned smile. 'I must seem like something of a copycat.'

'Not so far-fetched after all, eh?' Nagare said, smiling back at her.

'I just don't get it, though. I stayed up all night working on both those designs.'

'I suppose you've always carried your Amami heritage inside you.'

Saki straightened her posture. 'Sounds like something I should be proud of.'

'Oh, definitely,' said Koishi, beaming at her.

'It's funny. At first I had no idea why I'd even want to taste those noodles again. Now it all makes sense.' Saki's eyes were sparkling. 'Perhaps I should make a little trip to the island.'

'None of us are born into this world alone,' said Nagare. 'We each have a father and a mother, and they each had parents before them. Without them, we simply wouldn't be here.'

Saki reflected on this, then smiled cheerfully at the pair. 'To be honest, I've been in a bit of a creative rut recently. I made these brooches over a decade ago, and in the past year or so I've barely produced anything decent. This feels like the spark I've been waiting for.'

'Glad to hear it.' Nagare handed her the folder. 'I've written down recipes for both the noodles and the miki. Make them for your father sometime.'

'All the ingredients are in here,' said Koishi, holding out a paper bag.

'Thank you for everything.' Saki took the bag, then bowed and slid open the door. 'Oh!' she exclaimed, before retrieving her purse from her handbag. 'Almost forgot to pay.'

Koishi gave her their bank details, asking her simply to send them whatever felt right.

'Alright then. Thank you again.' Saki bowed once more, then set off west down Shomen-dori.

'You're not calling your driver?' Koishi called out from behind.

Saki turned back and smiled. ‘I think I’d like to walk a little first.’

‘Nice time of year for a stroll,’ murmured Nagare as they watched her depart.

Koishi turned to look at him. ‘Dad, people get married for the funniest of reasons, don’t they?’

‘Absolutely. There’s no predicting it. If there’s a connection, you end up together. And if not, well, that’s that.’

Back inside, Nagare glanced at the family altar.

‘Your mother and I were like that, you know. We had a real bond.’

Koishi hurried over to the altar, kneeled and put her hands together in prayer.

‘Like I said,’ Nagare went on, ‘we’re all connected. Parent to child, then to that child’s child, and so on and so forth. It continues long after we’re gone.’

He lit a stick of incense and set it in front of the altar.

Chapter 5:
Kara-Age

1

The Nozomi bullet train from Tokyo pulled into Kyoto station just after one in the afternoon. Masaru Suzuki made his way straight to the taxi stand, glancing only briefly at the hamburger stall he passed on the way. He was hungry enough, but he had somewhere to be.

He climbed into a taxi and showed the driver a map on which he'd marked his destination with a red cross. 'Here, please.'

'Ah, Shomen-dori,' replied the grey-haired driver, pushing up his glasses. 'Is it one of the altar shops?'

'No, it's a restaurant. The Kamogawa Diner.'

'Hmm.' The driver gave a doubtful tilt of his head, handed Masaru the map, and released the handbrake. 'Can't say I've heard of it.'

'Sorry to land you with such a short fare.'

The driver gave no reply as he pulled out. Maybe he was hard of hearing.

It was early December in Kyoto, hardly peak sightseeing season, and yet the streets were packed. It took them ten minutes just to leave the area around the station.

'We're lucky to have all these visitors,' said the driver, eyeing the crowds while they waited at a light. 'You here for the autumn leaves too?'

'No, I'm not here to sightsee. I didn't even know the leaves would still be on the trees at this time of year.'

'These days they last well into December. Must be that global warming.'

They crossed Shichijo-dori, and soon arrived on Shomen-dori. The driver slowed the vehicle and began glancing up and down the street.

'Here is fine,' said Masaru, reaching into his padded black briefcase for his wallet.

'If you're sure this is the spot,' said the driver, taking a thousand-yen bill and handing over the change. 'I can't see any restaurants . . .'

'Well, apparently not looking like one is part of the place's charm.'

Masaru hopped out of the taxi and immediately hunched his shoulders against the early-winter wind. He really should have worn a coat.

He was standing in front of a plain, two-storey mortar

building, with no sign, noren curtain or anything else suggesting that it was a restaurant. Confident that the details all matched the description he'd been given, he straightened his collar, adjusted his tie and nodded to himself.

'This is it, alright.'

As he reached for the door, a young man slid it open from inside, stepped out and called, 'See you next time!' into the interior.

The pair almost bumped into each other, but Masaru stepped politely aside and let the young man pass. He stepped through the doorway.

'Hello? My name is Masaru Suzuki. From Kanto Food Services. Is this the Kamogawa Diner?'

Hearing his loud, confident voice, a young woman in a sommelier's apron turned around. She glanced at his suit, then answered, a little bluntly, 'Sorry, but we don't take sales calls.'

'Ah, no, I'm not here to sell anything . . .'

As Masaru reached for his business card, a man in a loose-fitting samue emerged from the kitchen. 'You're Saburo's son, aren't you?'

'That's right. Masaru Suzuki. My father is very grateful for everything you've done for him.'

'Oh, we're the ones who're grateful. I'm Nagare Kamogawa, and this is my daughter Koishi.' He bowed, and Koishi followed suit. 'This gentleman's father runs a hot springs ryokan named Satsukitei, over in Kusatsu

Onsen,' Nagare explained to Koishi, his voice swelling with nostalgia. 'Your mother loved it there. It was right by the Yubatake, where all the hot water comes bubbling up in the middle of town. The baths were fantastic, of course, but it was the food that really stole our hearts. We used to drop by all the time – whatever the season.'

'We relocated three years ago, actually. We're a little further away from the Yubatake now.' Masaru smiled at Koishi, then handed Nagare a brochure for the ryokan.

'Your father was kind enough to invite us, but it's been hard to find the time to visit,' said Nagare, opening the brochure and scanning its pages.

Masaru glanced at the family altar in the living room, just visible through the curtain, on which stood a photograph of Kikuko. 'Mind if I pay my respects?'

'Please,' replied Nagare, showing him to the altar. 'You remember her, then?'

'Of course. I took her to see the crater lake at Mount Shirane. She was absolutely delighted.' Masaru joined Nagare in kneeling by the altar and joined his hands in prayer.

'I've heard all about this Satsukitei place,' said Koishi a little huffily, 'but no one's ever taken *me* there.'

'We'd love for you to come,' said Masaru. 'Why don't you pay us a visit some time? Your husband, too, if you—'

'I don't have one,' replied Koishi quickly, her nostrils flaring slightly.

'Sorry,' said Masaru, hurriedly bowing his head. 'I didn't mean to—'

'Koishi hasn't had much luck on that front,' said Nagare. 'Speaking of which, you're single, aren't you?' Nagare gave Masaru a look that managed to seem both playful and sincere.

'Oh, I . . .' Masaru had turned beetroot red. 'She'd be wasted on a country bumpkin like me.'

'Moving on,' said Nagare, getting to his feet, 'your father said you want our help recreating a dish. But he asked me to feed you first. I hope you're hungry.'

'That would be wonderful,' said Masaru, smiling as they returned to the restaurant. 'He said you serve the finest food in Kyoto.'

'Please, take a seat.' Koishi pulled out one of the red folding chairs, and Masaru eased himself into it.

'Lunch will be ready in no time,' said Nagare before trotting off to the kitchen.

'If you work for that food company, does that mean you're not taking over the ryokan?' asked Koishi, eyeing Masaru sideways as she poured him some tea.

'It's not really a food company in the usual sense,' said Masaru, raising the tall blue-and-white teacup to his lips. 'We provide consultancy services for the restaurant industry. I do plan on taking over the ryokan at some point. I'm just not sure when.'

'You must be a pro when it comes to cooking, then. Wouldn't it be faster for you to find this dish you're looking for on your own?'

'Oh, I'm hardly a pro. Just starting out, really.' Masaru took a slow sip of his tea.

'What exactly does a restaurant consultant do?'

'There are various different types, but I work on menu development – tasting dishes, giving feedback, that sort of thing. I'm more like an apprentice at the moment, though – I spend most of my time assisting senior consultants. It'll probably be another five years or so before they let me work on my own.'

Koishi refilled his cup. 'Well, I'm sure your father's ryokan will end up benefiting from all that expertise one day.'

'I'd like that,' said Masaru, before letting out a quiet sigh. 'But hospitality is a tricky old business.'

'Sorry to keep you waiting,' said Nagare, setting a rustic Shigaraki platter down in front of him. 'I've arranged everything on a single dish. I just hope it's enough for a young man like you.'

Masaru leaned forward, his eyes widening. 'This looks . . . incredible.'

'Shall I give you a rundown?'

'Please.'

'There are eight items in total. In the upper left is simmered Shogoin turnip, served with two types of miso: one infused with yuzu, the other with chilli. Next to that is the fugu sashimi millefeuille. There's ponzu jelly between the layers, so you can eat it as it is. The small bowl in the upper right is a miniature crab gratin – made with Echizen crab, and served with crushed Tartary buckwheat kernels, which you can sprinkle on top if you'd like. They add a nice crunch. As for the two dishes in the middle, the skewers on the right are duck meatballs, fried tsukune-style – try those with some sansho pepper and sweet vinegar. On the left is the grilled tilefish, which should go nicely with a sprinkle of seri parsley and roe salt. Finally, the bottom row. On the left is winter eel, grilled shirayaki-style without extra seasoning. Delicious wrapped in nori and dipped in the wasabi soy sauce. In the middle is deep-fried oyster, best enjoyed with a generous coating of the tartar sauce, which is made with suguki pickles. And on the right is Omi beef tenderloin, fried kara-age style. It's already seasoned, but a squeeze of the sudachi should add a nice citrus note.'

'Well,' said Masaru, surveying the contents of the platter in amazement. 'I had high expectations, and you've exceeded them. I can tell this is going to be . . . educational.'

'I forgot to ask,' said Koishi. 'Can I get you something to drink?'

'I know your father likes a tipple, but I hear it's not really your thing,' said Nagare. 'I guess it doesn't always run in the family.'

Masaru scratched the back of his head awkwardly. 'I've tried, believe me, but I'm a total lightweight.'

'No need to force yourself – it's just how you're built. How about a fine tea instead?' Nagare nodded to Koishi, who fetched a metal tea canister and tipped some leaves from it into a Banko pot.

'Today's rice dish is a softshell turtle porridge. Just let me know when you'd like it. In the meantime, enjoy!' Nagare bowed and made for the kitchen.

'I do wish I could serve you some sake with your meal,' said Koishi, pouring his tea into a tall Karatsu cup.

'Tell me about it,' replied Masaru, sipping the tea. 'I always feel like I'm missing out.'

'On the plus side, I guess tea lets you focus on the flavour of the food. Anyway – enjoy!' Koishi followed her father into the kitchen.

The restaurant fell silent. Left alone with the food, Masaru quietly cleared his throat, pressed his palms together in gratitude, and reached for his chopsticks.

He started with the shirayaki eel. They served plenty of eel at Satsukitei, too: paired with cucumber in a vinegared dish, rolled into omelettes, or on top of a bowl of rice at the end of a meal. It was a versatile enough ingredient, but one that rarely stole the spotlight. With no seasonal associations, everything depended on the chef's ability to make it shine.

As Nagare had instructed, he wrapped it in the toasted nori, dipped it in the wasabi soy sauce and took a bite. The eel was soft and warm, and its skin crisp, suggesting it had been grilled in the Kansai style.

People often avoided eel because it had the sharp fragrance common to river fish, and Masaru was usually one of them. Even when he enjoyed it, something about the aftertaste bothered him. When it was cooked kabayaki-style with sauce, he could just about bear it, but this was shirayaki, meaning there was no seasoning to mask the flavour. Masaru had always believed this to be a problem inherent in even the highest quality eel – but he was astonished by how clean and light this one tasted.

In fact, Masaru had never tasted eel like it. It had all the delicacy of white fish like sea bream or flounder, combined with the rich savour of yellowtail at the peak of its season. He had thought lightness and richness of flavour were two ends of a spectrum, that they couldn't possibly coexist – but this shirayaki proved otherwise.

Still in shock, he moved on to the fugu sashimi, and received another jolt of surprise.

Sashimi was an indispensable element of ryokan cuisine, but freshness was everything. Even with efficient modern distribution systems, a ryokan located far inland could never compete with one near the sea. That was the conclusion Masaru and his father Saburo had come to over the years.

Kusatsu Onsen was nearly a hundred kilometres from the Sea of Japan, and close to two hundred from the Pacific. At an altitude of twelve hundred metres, it was considered mountain country, which made seafood something of a hard sell. When Saburo had first taken over the ryokan, plenty of guests had muttered, 'Sashimi? In the mountains?'

Kyoto was a long way from the sea too, and when it came to the city's famed cuisine, fugu was hardly the first thing that came to mind. But the dish in front of Masaru surpassed even the versions he had eaten in places like Shimonoseki or Hakata, cities renowned for their pufferfish.

When you eat Nagare's food, empty your mind completely. That had been his father's advice. Taking it to heart, Masaru simply allowed his chopsticks to roam from one dish to the next, surrendering himself wholly to the act of eating.

'Is it all to your liking?' asked Nagare, arriving at his side.

'I'm honestly amazed. Stunned, in fact. I'm half tempted to ask you to take me on as an apprentice.' Masaru's expression, like Nagare's earlier, managed to seem both playful and sincere.

'Oh, please. This pales in comparison to your father's cooking. Compared to him I'm just an amateur.'

'Seriously. I can't even fathom how you've achieved these flavours.' Masaru was staring with grave intensity at the near-empty platter.

'I figured you might still be hungry, so I've brought

some yakisoba before the rice course,' said Nagare, setting a square dish down beside the platter. Fragrant steam rose through the air.

Masaru leaned over the plate. 'This is yakisoba?'

'My take on kawara soba, which I had in Yamaguchi once. The noodles are matcha soba instead of the usual Chinese type. Dip them in the tsuyu sauce the way you would with regular soba.'

The square grey plate was heaped with dark green, slightly charred noodles, topped with shredded omelette and thin slivers of pork.

'You can drop that slice of lemon into the sauce if you'd like. Eat up while it's still hot!'

As Nagare returned to the kitchen, Masaru eagerly started on the noodles. He'd heard of this dish, a specialty from Kawatana Onsen in Yamaguchi, but this was the first time he'd laid eyes on it in person. The idea of pairing stir-fried noodles with a dipping sauce struck him as entirely novel. After his first mouthful, he added the lemon garnish to the sauce as Nagare had suggested.

Masaru had only ever eaten yakisoba with the usual thick brown sauce mixed in, or sometimes with a lighter, salt-based sauce. He'd never even imagined eating it like this. *This could easily work as part of a kaiseki meal at Satsukitei*, he thought as he emptied the plate.

What impressed him most of all, though, was Nagare's

thoughtfulness. It was true that the large platter hadn't quite sated his appetite, even with the promise of rice to follow. But if he'd been served the yakisoba earlier, it would have distracted from the main dishes. The portions, the timing – everything had been carefully calibrated with the customer in mind.

All that remained was to sprinkle some sansho pepper onto the duck meatballs, roll them in the sweet vinegar and chew away. Before long, the large platter was empty, too.

Soon, Nagare emerged from the kitchen bearing a small clay pot.

'Here's the rice porridge. Watch out – it's hot.'

Nagare set the pot down on a mat and lifted the lid, unleashing a thick cloud of steam.

'What a fragrance!' exclaimed Masaru, smiling dreamily as the vapour rose around him.

'More like risotto than your usual rice porridge. Probably easiest to eat it with a spoon. There should be some crispy bits of rice stuck to the bottom – scrape them up if you like.'

'Did you say it was made with softshell turtle? How decadent . . . And what are these?' Masaru pointed at the small glass dish and cup by the pot.

'Finely chopped green sansho peppercorns and freshly squeezed ginger. Try mixing them in halfway through, and notice how the flavours shift. Should keep things interesting. I'll leave this teapot here with you, too.'

Masaru nodded eagerly, then dipped his spoon into the clay pot.

The porridge was steaming hot and, as Nagare had said, more like risotto in texture. The individual grains of rice were still intact, but soft all the way through. While the broth was unmistakeably Japanese, there was something faintly Western in there too. Masaru couldn't even begin to imagine how Nagare had crafted such flavours.

He specialized in menu development, albeit as a junior consultant, and yet he couldn't identify a single seasoning or technique that had been used. It all seemed too complex to grasp. Even so, his frustration was mingled with a kind of exhilaration.

The clay pot was small, but the porridge turned out to be more than substantial. The yakisoba had packed quite a punch, too. By the time he scraped up the last of the crunchy rice, he was about ready to burst.

'Did I give you enough?' asked Nagare.

'More than,' replied Masaru, patting his swollen belly.

'Good, good. You take a breather, and then I'll show you through.'

'Sorry I took so long to eat,' said Masaru as they walked down the corridor. 'When the food's that good, you can't help but slow down and enjoy it. I'm usually so busy with work that I just wolf things down.'

'It's easy to eat too quickly, especially when you don't have any sake to sip on. But you're right: food is meant to be savoured.'

'Did you make all these dishes?' asked Masaru, gazing at the photos lining the corridor.

'For the most part. A few I came across on my travels. In fact, there should be a photo from Satsukitei somewhere.' Nagare stopped and stretched up on his toes as he searched for the photo.

'Oh, there's no need to dig it out,' said Masaru, stepping past Nagare. 'It'll only be embarrassing.'

'Here we are. Kikuko found one of the dishes so tasty she asked for another helping, and then your father came to say hello. That's when we took this.'

The slightly faded photo showed one of the guest rooms at Satsukitei. Nagare and Kikuko sat facing each other across a low table, while Saburo was kneeling at one side. But the most crucial part of the scene – the food – was hard to make out.

'What was the dish she liked so much?' asked Masaru, leaning in close.

'Finely shredded cabbage. Served with the Joshu beef teriyaki. She swore it was one of the best things she'd ever eaten. Practically begged for more of it.' Nagare chuckled softly and began walking again.

'Just . . . shredded cabbage?' Masaru froze for a moment in disbelief, then scrambled to catch up.

'Koishi will take it from here,' said Nagare, opening the door at the end of the corridor.

Koishi looked up and greeted him. 'Come on in.'

'Hello again.' Masaru stepped somewhat hesitantly into the office, then filled out the form she handed him.

'Masaru Suzuki,' said Koishi, scanning his answers. 'Twenty-six. So young! Still living the life of a bachelor, then?'

'Yes.' A faint smile flickered across Masaru's face. 'I, er, haven't had much luck in that department.'

Koishi smiled back, then opened her notebook. 'So, what's the dish you want help with?'

'Kara-age,' said Masaru, and his voice seemed to crack slightly.

'Ooh, deep-fried chicken? I'm a big fan.' She readied her pen. 'When and where did you eat this particular kara-age?'

'I was in my final year of high school. I had it at a place in Kusatsu called Tori-dake. Tori as in "chicken", and dake as in "mountain".'

'And you were seventeen or eighteen at the time . . . making this what, eight years ago? I'm guessing the restaurant is gone now.'

Masaru nodded silently in response.

'So, what about this kara-age stood out?'

'That's the thing. It wasn't distinctive in any obvious way – just unbelievably tasty. It was pre-seasoned, but you ate it with this sort of . . . sauce.' Masaru's eyes shone. 'I've never had kara-age like it.'

'Hmm. Kara-age doesn't tend to vary much from place to place, but dipping it in sauce does sound unusual. And did you only visit Tori-dake that one time?'

'Actually, I ate there almost every day.'

Koishi's eyes widened dramatically. 'You had the kara-age every day?'

'No, no – normally I just had onigiri. I only got to try the kara-age once.'

'Really? But it was a local restaurant, right? And with a name like that, wasn't chicken the specialty?'

'It was. But the kara-age itself was more of a rumour than a dish.' Masaru paused, as if hesitating to go on. 'It's a long story. Do you mind?'

'Listening to long stories is my job.'

'Most hot-spring ryokans are in business pretty much year-round, twenty-four hours a day. And, our place being family-run, it was almost unheard of for us all to have dinner together.'

'I can relate,' said Koishi in a subdued voice. 'We almost never had the whole family around the table when I was a kid.'

'My mum worked at the ryokan too, and she came home late at night. She'd only cook dinner when she got in, so as a kid I was always hungry. In high school I had baseball practice every afternoon, and there was no way I was going to wait that long to eat. I got into the habit of dropping by Tori-dake with my teammates after practice.'

'I'm not surprised. You must have been famished. Did they make the onigiri extra large for you?'

'Absolutely. Old Mr Kawakami used to call them "rice bombs".'

'Ah,' said Koishi, jotting down the name. 'Was he the owner?'

'Yes. Zenzo Kawakami.' Masaru lowered his voice. 'I heard he died a few years ago, not long after shutting up shop and moving out of town.'

Koishi folded her arms pensively. 'If the restaurant's gone, and the owner's passed away, this might be tricky.'

'Sorry.'

'I guess we'll have to track down other people who tried this kara-age and see what they tell us.'

'I thought of that too. The problem is, it isn't that simple.'

'How come? If it was the restaurant's specialty, lots of people must have eaten it.'

'Like I said, it was more of a sort of myth. It wasn't even on the menu. There were just rumours. I never actually met anyone else who'd eaten it.'

'I'm not sure I follow. Can you tell me a bit more about the restaurant?'

'It was a casual sort of place, not far from the Yubatake. During the day they served all sorts – udon, soba, ramen, rice bowls, curry – and at night they switched to yakitori. It was always packed with tourists and employees from all the ryokan, but I never saw kara-age on the menu.'

'Why, I wonder? You'd think it would have been their main offering!'

'I've no idea. Mr Kawakami was a quiet man. I hardly ever talked to him.'

'I can just picture it. The gruff old master grilling yakitori in silence.'

'Sounds about right. Though I didn't go there in the evening, so I never tried the yakitori.'

'I have another question for you. If Mr Kawakami served ramen and rice bowls and all sorts of other things, why stick to onigiri?'

'It was the only thing he'd serve me.'

'How come?'

'He wanted me to eat dinner properly when I got home. Told me to think of my poor mother, working hard all day at the inn and then coming home to cook. He said eating any other dish that late in the day would be disrespectful to her.'

'Wise words. I remember doing just that – eating a bowl of instant ramen because I couldn't wait for Mum to get home, then not being able to finish the dinner she made me. She looked heartbroken.' Koishi's gaze softened. 'This Mr Kawakami sounds like a good man.'

'Back then I thought it was a little unfair, but looking back he was right,' said Masaru reflectively. 'If he'd served me ramen or curry, I doubt dinner would have tasted half as good as it did.'

'So, if the onigiri was just to tide you over, then this kara-age must have been for some special occasion. Your birthday, maybe?'

'The baseball team at Kusatsu Chuo High was, well, not the greatest. We'd won a grand total of two interschool games in our entire history, and those were over twenty years ago. In the three years I'd been on the team, we hadn't managed to change that record.' Masaru's voice quivered with regret. 'Mr Kawakami told us he'd make us kara-age if we won. It became our motivation. But we just couldn't break the spell.'

'Sounds tough.'

'Whenever we dropped by Tori-dake after losing another game, we'd sit there chewing on our onigiri in silence. Berating ourselves for being such disappointments.'

'Sounds about as cheerful as a funeral.'

'Yeah,' replied Masaru softly. 'Something like that.'

'Ah, now I get it. You finally got your first win in twenty years, and Mr Kawakami made you the kara-age to celebrate?'

'Unfortunately not.' Masaru stared down at the table. 'We ended up losing the final match of our senior year, too.'

Koishi let out a quiet sigh. 'Right.'

'The atmosphere was even gloomier than usual that day, so the captain suggested we skip our usual trip to Tori-dake. But in the end it felt like we should still drop by and let Mr Kawakami know. When we walked in and told him, he marched off into the kitchen without a word. We were expecting the usual "rice bombs", but instead he turned up with this mountain of freshly fried chicken. Even though we'd lost!'

'He wanted to cheer you up,' said Koishi, tears welling in her eyes. 'He sounds like a real angel.'

'Normally he barely said a word, but that day he looked us in the eyes and said, "You can lose as many matches as you want, boys. Just don't lose at life. Live it with your heads held high." '

'Good advice if ever I heard it.'

'Yes, but what really stuck with me was what he said next.' Masaru gazed into space as he went on. 'He gave us this pained look, then told us that he was speaking from experience. That he knew what it meant to lose at life.'

'Losing at life, eh . . .' said Koishi, following his gaze. 'I feel like I can relate to that, too.'

Masaru smiled weakly. 'My dad used to say something similar.'

'I forgot to ask. What made you want to eat this kara-age again all of a sudden?'

'Well, it's not just the kara-age per se. I want to reconnect with what Mr Kawakami told us. Ever since I took my current job, I've felt like I'm stuck in an endless losing streak. Just like back then.' Masaru seemed to be fighting back tears. 'What I mean is, I'm starting to feel like I'm losing at life, too.'

'Right,' said Koishi. 'Well, we'll get right on the case. Don't you worry.'

He glanced up at her, and she smiled back.

Back in the restaurant, Nagare was perched at the counter. He had been leafing through a photo album, but snapped it shut as the pair returned.

'Did the interview go okay?' he asked.

'Yes,' replied Masaru. 'Koishi was very patient with me.'

'Whatever you're looking for, we'll give it our best shot.'

'This is a tough one, Dad,' said Koishi, glancing at Masaru.

Nagare narrowed his eyes. 'You always say that.'

'So,' Masaru cut in, 'when should I come back?'

'How about in a fortnight or so?' replied Nagare.

'Of course.' Masaru adjusted his collar. 'Just let me know a couple of days in advance and I'll get permission from my company.'

'My regards to your father,' said Nagare with a grin. Masaru smiled back, then made his way out of the restaurant. After seeing him off, Koishi and Nagare sat down at the counter.

'What's he after, then?' asked Nagare.

'Kara-age.'

'Kara-age, eh? Made by his parents?'

'No, at a restaurant in Kusatsu Onsen. Long gone, of course.'

'Naturally. He wouldn't have come to us otherwise.'

'Dad . . .'

'Hey,' said Nagare, flinching slightly. 'Why are you staring at me like that?'

'I want to visit this Satsukitei place. Mum was always saying she wanted to go back there one last time.'

'Koishi, don't get any funny ideas,' said Nagare sternly. 'Our job is to track down this kara-age. Not go lounging about at a ryokan.'

'I know, I know. But Mr Suzuki's family runs the place, right? You never know what clues I might stumble across!'

'When did you get so good at twisting my arm? Fine, I'll leave this one up to you. As long as you're sure you're up to the task.'

'Don't you worry, Dad. I'll search high and low. Just . . . let me go to Kusatsu.'

'No slacking off, you hear?'

Koishi threw her arms around him. 'Thanks, Dad!'

2

With the New Year fast approaching, Kyoto station was deserted, and there were almost no tourists in sight. Masaru followed an underground passage from the Hachijo-dori exit, where the taxis waited, to the central exit on the station's north side. He'd taken a taxi to the restaurant last time, but on the way back had realized it'd be quicker to walk from the central exit.

This time he was dressed casually, in jeans, a sweater and a loose-fitting jacket. He walked north up Karasuma-dori, crossed Shichijo-dori, then turned east down Shomen-dori.

When he slid open the door to the restaurant, it appeared to be empty.

'Hello?' he called. 'It's Masaru.'

Nagare stepped out of the kitchen, removed his cap and bowed. 'Good to see you again.'

Masaru bowed back. 'I'm really looking forward to this.'

'Sorry we ended up taking so long.'

'Not at all – I'm the one who should apologize for putting you to so much trouble,' said Masaru, slipping off his jacket and hanging it on a chair. 'Anyway, we're a lot less busy around the New Year, so this has actually worked out well.'

'It's all my fault,' said Koishi, emerging from the kitchen and bowing. 'I made a bit of a mess of things.'

Nagare shot her a glance. 'I asked her to go to Kusatsu, but she came back empty-handed. Ended up having to make a trip of my own.'

'I'm so grateful to your parents. They really spoiled me,' said Koishi, her gaze dropping to the floor. 'But I just couldn't crack the case.'

'I really am sorry for asking the impossible,' said Masaru.

'Actually, I think we just about managed it,' said Nagare. 'No guarantees, though. Just . . . eat it and see what you think, okay? I'll get it ready now.'

'Thank you very much.' Masaru took a seat. It was only

his second time at the restaurant, and yet he felt oddly nostalgic about the place. Maybe because it reminded him of Tori-dake. Up on a hanging shelf, next to a small TV, was a miniature Shinto shrine complete with talismanic strips of paper, together with one of the decorative bamboo branches seen at this time of year. The end table was strewn with magazines and newspapers. Despite this slightly jumbled interior, the restaurant didn't feel messy at all – if anything, it gave the impression of having been meticulously cleaned. There wasn't a speck of dust on the floor, and whenever he glimpsed the stainless-steel surfaces in the kitchen they seemed to gleam like mirrors.

It was a level of cleanliness uncommon in a casual restaurant – and it was this, more than anything, that reminded Masaru of Tori-dake. Whenever Mr Kawakami had a spare moment, he'd spend it diligently polishing his stoves or worktops. Masaru could still see the stern look on his face as he did so.

The distinctive aroma of deep-fried food began drifting in from the kitchen, making Masaru even hungrier than he already was. When the sizzle of oil reached his ears, his stomach growled impatiently.

'Sorry for the wait.' Nagare set a pair of bamboo chopsticks down on a ceramic rest.

Masaru took a deep breath. 'I feel kind of nervous.'

'It'll be ready in just a moment.' Nagare glanced over at the kitchen, then set down a small blue-and-white dish filled with a brown sauce.

'Hojicha should pair nicely with the meal.' Koishi set a Mashiko teapot and Shigaraki teacup down on the table together with a glass of water, then returned to the kitchen.

After a while, Masaru heard the sizzle of oil again. Was Nagare frying it a second time?

The sizzling grew gradually quieter until it was almost inaudible.

'Here we are. Enjoy it while it's hot.'

Nagare set two white Western-style plates down on the table. They were heaped with fried chicken.

Masaru took a deep sniff. 'Smells amazing.'

'The ones on the right have the bones still in. On the left is boneless. Eat them as they are, or dip them in the sauce. You can sprinkle a bit of pepper into the sauce too, if you like. I'll bring some rice out in a moment.'

No sooner had Nagare stepped away from the table than Masaru grabbed his chopsticks and retrieved a piece of karaage from the right-hand dish.

Just like he had back then.

When Mr Kawakami first set the huge plate of kara-age down in front of them, it had startled them into silence. Then he gave the signal – 'Go on then, dig in' – and their hands all shot out at once.

The pieces of kara-age were so hot, and so enormous, that they almost burned their mouths. But as they chomped away, the grins on their faces only grew wider.

'Watch out for those bones,' Mr Kawakami had warned them. 'Unless you want to break a tooth, that is,' he added, prompting a ripple of laughter.

'Try some of this,' he said, setting down a bowl of sauce which he sprinkled liberally with pepper.

Some of them ate the kara-age as it was, as if they couldn't bear to waste any time that might be spent eating; others did as the chef had suggested, dipping the chicken in the sauce and spluttering slightly as they ate.

Before they knew it, the sting of losing that final game had all but vanished. And when, in no time at all, they demolished the mountain of kara-age, Mr Kawakami immediately returned with another platter piled just as high as the first.

'This batch is boneless, so go wild.'

This time, perhaps because they were in less of a hurry, they all began dunking the chicken in the sauce.

For a moment, Masaru could have sworn he was sitting in Tori-dake, surrounded by the excited shouts of his teammates.

Still, there was no guarantee it would taste the same. The circumstances were just too different. That day, to Masaru and his dejected teammates, the arrival of the platter of kara-age had been like stumbling across an oasis in the middle of a desert.

He reached for one of the boneless pieces, dipped it in the peppery sauce, then took a bite.

The crunch. The rush of hot juices. The deep savour of the sauce . . . Any remaining doubts had been obliterated. This was the kara-age he'd eaten that day.

'So, did we get it right?' asked Nagare, setting a Tobe bowl heaped with rice in front of him.

Masaru nodded firmly. 'My memories were a little hazy at first, but it's all come back to me now. This is it. This is the kara-age I ate at Tori-dake.'

'Excellent. Should be even better with some rice.'

'Thanks,' said Masaru, grinning bashfully. 'I was just thinking I could use some.'

'How are you for tea?' asked Koishi, lifting the lid of the earthenware teapot and peering in. It was still brimming with hojicha.

'The chicken's so tasty, I forgot all about it.' Masaru

shook his head in disbelief. 'I just can't get my head around this. How on earth did you pull it off?'

'Dad will reveal all in a moment, but let me tell you, he really pulled out all the stops. He ended up going all the way to Hokkaido!'

'That's enough chatter, Koishi,' said Nagare sternly. 'Let him enjoy his meal in peace.' Koishi responded with a playful shrug.

'I look forward to hearing all about it,' said Masaru, smiling and nodding. 'For now, I'll just focus on how good it tastes.'

Koishi and Nagare disappeared back through the kitchen curtain.

Masaru worked his way through the rest of the chicken, alternating between the two plates and pausing occasionally to sip on his tea.

How many times had he eaten kara-age since that day at Tori-dake? Between work and his personal life, more than he could say. Yet when it came to versions of the dish that had really stuck with him, he could have counted them on one hand.

Meanwhile, this kara-age was so distinctive that it made comparisons meaningless. On top of that, it felt like one of those rare flavours you'd never grow tired of.

Still, even if Nagare told him the recipe, he didn't see how any of this would help him at work. It certainly wouldn't end his losing streak. As he coated the last piece of chicken in the sauce, set it on his rice and wolfed it down, Masaru began to wonder why he'd come looking for the kara-age in the first place.

Having emptied the two white plates, he noticed that they were lined with oil-absorbing washi paper. It bore only the faintest traces of grease. How had Nagare managed to drain the oil so thoroughly? Masaru reached for one of the plates and studied it closely.

Nagare returned from the kitchen and, as if reading Masaru's thoughts, said, 'There's not much to it, you know.'

Masaru set the plate back down. 'I just can't figure it out.'

'Mind if I join you?' asked Nagare, gesturing to the seat on the other side of the laminated table.

'Please. I'm dying to know the big secret.'

'Oh, I wouldn't call it a secret.'

'You went all the way to Hokkaido, then? I really can't thank you enough.' Masaru bowed from his seat.

'From what I hear, we should be thanking you,' said Nagare drily. 'Koishi told me she got a very warm welcome at Satsukitei. Sounds like she really made the most of the hot springs, too.'

'But what took you all the way to Hokkaido?'

'Well, when Koishi arrived in Kusatsu, she found that Tori-dake had vanished without a trace, and no one in the neighbourhood seemed to know where Mr Kawakami had moved. He didn't seem to have any family, either. Koishi had hit a dead end, so there was nothing for it: I followed my gut. The name Tori-dake reminded me of something, see. So I flew up to Kushiro.' Nagare unfolded a map of the northern island of Hokkaido on the table. The city of Kushiro lay on its eastern edge.

'Why Kushiro?' asked Masaru, looking down at the map and then back at Nagare.

'Are you familiar with a dish called zangi?'

'Zangi . . . it does ring a bell.' Suzuki clutched his head as if trying to think. 'What is it again?'

'It's what they call heavily seasoned kara-age in Hokkaido. There are all sorts of theories about the name's origins, though none of them have been proven. In any case, the restaurant where it's supposed to have originated is in Kushiro. A place, as it happens, called Tori-take – the second half of the name being the character for "bamboo" rather than "mountain". I thought there might be a connection with the Kusatsu place, so I went to check it out.' Nagare laid out the photos he'd taken at the Kushiro restaurant.

'Tori-dake and Tori-take, eh? They do sound similar. Wait. This kara-age is . . .' Masaru reached for the photo of the fried chicken.

'Identical.' said Nagare, leaning across the table to look at the photo. 'What you just ate is actually a recreation of the version served at Tori-take.'

Masaru looked up. 'But . . . why?'

'The clue was that sauce. There are all sorts of kara-age in this country, but very few that use a dipping sauce. The zangi at Kushiro is one of them. They even have a special name for the sauce: zan-tare. I guessed that might be what we were looking for. Then there was the fact that the two restaurants had such similar names.'

'I can't believe you thought of looking somewhere as far away as Hokkaido,' said Masaru, shaking his head in awe. 'I guess that's what you call thinking outside of the box.'

Nagare gave a wry grin. 'I tend to trust my instincts. Not that they're always right, of course, but this time they served me well. It turns out that some thirty years ago, Mr Kawakami worked at Tori-take. He was on good terms with the owner, Mr Sakakura – and practically his right-hand man. One day, he got into a quarrel with a customer. Things grew heated, and eventually the police were involved. Worried he'd tarnished the restaurant's name, Mr Kawakami quit and moved out of town. For the next five years or so, he wrote occasional letters to Mr Sakakura, but eventually even those stopped coming. When I explained that he'd started a restaurant called Tori-dake in Kusatsu, Mr Sakakura was deeply moved.'

'I had . . . no idea,' murmured Masaru.

'The fact that Mr Kawakami named his restaurant after

Tori-take suggests he still felt conflicted about everything that had happened. That would also explain why he refused to put kara-age on the menu.'

'So when he served it to us that day, he was breaking his own rule. Why, though?'

'Who knows? Maybe he saw something of himself in you,' said Nagare with a faint smile. 'Pure speculation on my part, of course.'

'Are you able to tell me the recipe?'

'I'm not sure if you can even call it a recipe, but yes, I've written down the basic steps. Mr Sakakura showed me the whole process. You cut the chicken into bite-size pieces, season with salt, pepper and a marinade, coat them in potato starch flour, and fry them in lard. When they turn golden-brown, they're ready to be served – with a Worcestershire-sauce-based dip on the side. That's all there is to it.'

'But there must be some special ingredient in the marinade or the sauce, right?' said Masaru, dipping a finger into the leftover sauce and tasting it.

'Mr Sakakura insisted he didn't use anything out of the ordinary.'

'Really? Well, if I used premium free-range chicken, made the sauce a little spicier and marketed this as a "secret recipe", I think I might be onto a winner. Thank you so much. This might just save my career.'

Masaru's cheeks had flushed with excitement, but Nagare rose from the table and looked away.

'I knew coming here was the right call,' Masaru went on breathlessly. 'I'll start pitching it to my clients right away.'

'Very well,' replied Nagare in an oddly detached tone as he handed him a paper bag. 'You'll find the basic recipe and a sample of the sauce in here.'

'Thank you. Now, can I pay?' Masaru reached for his wallet.

'Koishi?' Nagare called towards the kitchen. 'All done in there?'

Koishi stepped out, wiping her hands with a towel.

'He'd like to pay,' Nagare explained, now visibly frowning.

Koishi handed Masaru a slip of paper. 'We let the client choose the fee, for both the meal and the detective services. Just send us whatever feels right.'

'Certainly,' he replied, folding the paper neatly and tucking it into his wallet. 'This could be the start of something big for me. I'll be sure to reward you generously for everything you've done.'

As he was making to leave, Nagare blocked his path, looked him in the eye, and said, 'Mr Suzuki.'

Masaru took a half-step backwards, alarm showing on his face. 'Y-yes?'

'Do you remember what Kikuko asked for an extra helping of? At Satsukitei, I mean.'

'Yes. The shredded cabbage, you said.'

'That's right. Plain old shredded cabbage. Now, why do you think she asked for a second portion of something so simple?'

Masaru gave him a puzzled look. 'Well . . . because it was tasty?'

'Exactly. Because it was tasty. But do you know *why* it was so tasty?'

'This is starting to feel like one of those Zen riddles,' said Masaru impatiently. 'Things are tasty because they're tasty, aren't they?'

'A few days before that trip to Satsukitei, Kikuko's wisdom tooth swelled right up and she had it pulled,' explained Nagare, his gaze wandering off into the middle distance. 'We chatted about it while we were enjoying the appetizers, and the maid happened to overhear. She said she'd ask the chef to make Kikuko's dishes nice and soft so as not to bother the wound.'

Masaru's eyes widened. 'Even the cabbage?'

'Softening it up with a little salt, while keeping the crunch – that's no easy feat. I think Kikuko was moved by how perfectly the chef pulled it off. Asking for seconds was her way of saying thank you. Your father picked up on that, which is why he dropped by our room in person. And that's how we became friends.'

Masaru simply stared at him, waiting for him to go on.

'That's what good food is about. Fancy ingredients and secret sauces might linger in the mind, but they're not what touches your heart. What matters in this business is what you can really *do* for your customer – how you connect with them on a deep, emotional level. Yes, the kara-age you ate at Tori-dake tasted good. But that sensation didn't come from your tongue or your stomach. It came from in here.' Nagare set a hand on his heart. His eyes seemed to have reddened slightly.

'One more thing,' he went on. 'Keep in mind that zangi only came about because of the development of broiler chicken after the war. Suddenly, chicken was much easier to obtain, and people started racking their brains for tasty but inexpensive ways of cooking it. Zangi was the result. Back then, there were no nitpicking food critics, or fancy branded types of chicken. No special ingredients, no secret sauces – just simple, tasty food that everyone could enjoy.' Nagare let out a long sigh. 'Times have certainly changed.'

'Thank you,' said Masaru, bowing deeply. 'There I was, about to march off in completely the wrong direction. I'll never forget what you've just told me.'

'Glad to hear it,' said Nagare, his expression softening.

Koishi slid open the door. 'It's cold outside, so take care. And if you see your parents, please give them my best.'

'I will,' said Masaru, his lips pressed together resolutely. 'And I'll be sure to tell them what you taught me today, too.'

As he stepped outside, a tabby cat sauntered over. Masaru crouched down to stroke its head. 'Is this your cat?'

Koishi squatted at his side. 'Not really *ours*, per se. But we have given him a name: Drowsy. Mainly because he spends most of his life sleeping.'

'Drowsy, eh?' said Masaru, slowly getting to his feet. 'Must be nice. Napping all day. Never wondering about whether he's winning or losing.'

'Mr Suzuki, life isn't a game of baseball,' said Nagare. 'The score isn't that easy to read. If anything, it's an endless series of tiny victories and tiny defeats – and there's no telling which is coming for you next.'

Masaru nodded in agreement, bowed and set off west down Shomen-dori. The cat went padding after him.

'Don't go too far, Drowsy,' called Koishi. 'You'll get lost.' Drowsy responded by plopping himself down on the spot.

They watched Masaru disappear down the street, then stepped back inside.

'Glad that's all settled,' said Koishi. 'I haven't seen you look that scary in a long time.'

'Couldn't let him leave without clearing that up,' replied

Nagare, sitting at the counter and unfolding a newspaper. 'His parents would never forgive me.'

'Dad,' said Koishi from behind.

He turned to face her, newspaper still open in his hands. 'What is it?'

Koishi stepped into the kitchen and faced the family altar, tears glistening in her eyes. 'I wish the three of us could have stayed at Satsukitei sometime. You know, when I was there, I kept having this image of us all sleeping side by side in that tatami room.'

Nagare set his newspaper down and came to join her in gazing at the portrait of Kikuko. 'We never imagined that would be her last trip.'

'Oh, I think she knew,' said Koishi, lighting a stick of incense. 'That was why she wanted it just to be the two of you.'

'Maybe. She spent the whole time grumbling about this and that, you know. Probably saw it as her last chance to get things off her chest.'

'Yeah. That sounds like her.'

Kneeling by the altar, Koishi and Nagare pressed their palms together in unison.

Chapter 6: Macaroni Gratin

1

Yuiko Tomita stepped out of Kyoto station's central exit, took a moment to gaze up at the looming form of Kyoto Tower, then strode confidently off along Karasuma-dori.

With only a light jacket to shield her from the icy winds racing down from Mount Hiei, Yuiko hardly looked like a woman approaching sixty. Her neatly cropped black hair gave her a look of girlish innocence, while her beige two-piece hinted at a quiet, professional resolve.

She had visited Kyoto countless times with friends, but today was different. In fact – she noticed as she waited at a pedestrian crossing – the city's very air seemed somehow altered.

She hurried across Shichijo-dori, continued north up Karasuma-dori, then turned east onto Shomen-dori. Soon enough, her destination came into view.

A two-storey mortar-walled building, with no sign or

other indication that it was a restaurant; her only clue the enticing fragrances wafting into the street. It was all just as she'd expected. She smiled, then twitched her nostrils. Was that dashi stock she could smell?

Yuiko took a deep breath, then slid open the door.

'Hello?'

'Can I help?' a young woman in a sommelier's apron asked over her shoulder.

'Is this the Kamogawa Detective Agency?' Yuiko asked with some trepidation.

The woman's face creased into a smile. 'It is. I'm the head of the agency, Koishi Kamogawa. Would you happen to be Ms Tomita?'

Yuiko shifted her black tote to her other hand and smiled back. 'That's me – Yuiko Tomita. I'm here on Akane Daidoji's recommendation.'

An older man in a loose samue emerged from the kitchen and bowed. 'Akane let me know you'd be dropping by.'

Yuiko bowed deeply. 'Yes, she told me all about this place. It's a pleasure to meet you both.'

'Take a seat,' said Koishi, pulling out a chair. Yuiko removed her jacket and did as instructed.

'Koishi will speak to you in a moment about this dish you're looking for – but first, lunch. I'll just get a few things ready.' Nagare slipped back into the kitchen.

'Can I get you a drink?' asked Koishi.

'I'm not a big drinker, but I am partial to a good sake.'

'I could fetch you one I've been enjoying recently. Hoju, it's called. From Hiroshima. Tastes amazing warmed up.'

'Hiroshima, eh? I'd love to try it. Just a little is fine, though – really.' Yuiko held her thumb and forefinger a fraction apart to demonstrate.

'I'll warm you up a small flask.' Koishi trotted off to the kitchen.

Yuiko glanced around the now-silent restaurant. It looked just like the casual shokudo eateries her father had taken her to as a little girl. She remembered taking half an hour to finish a single bowl of udon, her father hurrying her all the while.

'Shabby old place, isn't it?' said Koishi, grinning as she set down a reddish-brown Bizen sake flask and cup in front of her.

'It's funny,' said Yuiko, cupping the warm flask with both hands. 'I've never been here before, but it feels strangely familiar.'

'It gets seriously draughty in the winter, and the heating barely works,' said Koishi, before giving her a mischievous look. 'So the only way to warm ourselves up is with sake.'

'You sound like a seasoned drinker.'

'My mum always used to say I got it from Dad.'

Seeing Koishi glance at the family altar in the adjoining room, Yuiko bowed her head politely.

'By the way,' Koishi went on, studying Yuiko closely, 'if you don't mind me asking, how old are you? You don't look anything like the age Akane mentioned.'

It was true: there wasn't a trace of grey in her short, cropped hair, and there was something almost un-Japanese about her striking, well-defined features.

'I'm fifty-seven, I swear. I've just had a few . . . tweaks along the way,' said Yuiko, smiling wryly as she pointed at her eyes and nose. 'You could say this isn't quite the real me.'

'Tweaks. As in—'

'Plastic surgery, yes. I had my reasons. It was a long time ago. My father gave me hell for it.'

Koishi tilted her head to one side and leaned in slightly. 'Well, for what it's worth, it's very . . . professional. You look younger than me! Maybe I should get some work done myself.'

'I wouldn't if I were you,' replied Yuiko, a vaguely sorrowful look crossing her features. 'It might just change your whole life.'

'Sorry for the wait,' said Nagare, arriving with a three-tiered wooden steamer, which he set down in front of Yuiko. 'Given the chilly weather we've been having, I've focused on hot dishes.'

Yuiko glanced up at him. 'I feel warmer just looking at them!'

'I'll run you through everything,' said Nagare, removing the lid and setting each tier of the steamer on a separate white plate in front of her.

Yuiko's eyes sparkled as she took in the spread. 'I hope I can finish all this.'

'It looks like a lot, but the portions are actually quite small. There are three dishes in each steamer. In the first one, on the left, you have sawara mackerel, grilled Kyoto-style in a white miso marinade, simmered Shogoin turnip, and softshell turtle in a savoury steamed custard. In the middle steamer: slices of duck breast layered with namafu – wheat-gluten cake, that is – to be enjoyed with the mustard paste. Next to that is the steamed oyster – it was on the large side, so I've sliced it up for you. Try that with some of the grated daikon and chilli. And a steamed crab terrine, served with a yuzu gelée. In the third steamer: Omi beef-tongue stew, simmered with a blend of white and red miso. You'll want a spoon for that. The middle dish is steamed fugu, which you can garnish with the minced negi onions and a dash of ponzu. Finally, on the right: kuruma prawn wrapped in tofu skin and lightly seared. Nice with a sprinkle of matcha salt.'

Yuiko gripped her chopsticks and let out an admiring sigh. 'What a feast. I don't think I've eaten any of these dishes before.'

'Since they're all warm dishes, here are some pickles

as a palate cleanser,' Nagare went on, setting down three small bowls. 'The yellowish one is suguki, the white one is Shogoin turnip, and the purple one is shibazuke: aubergine, cucumber and ginger mixed with red perilla leaves. All minced quite finely, so use a spoon for those, too. I'll bring some rice through in a moment.'

'Just let me know if you need more of that sake,' said Koishi, before following her father into the kitchen.

Yuiko studied the three steamers once more, then replaced the lids on those on either side and pulled the middle one towards her. After a quick sip of the sake, she poured the yuzu gelée over the steamed crab terrine and brought it to her lips.

'Wow,' she gasped, almost involuntarily.

The warm meat was delicate and sweet, while the gelée added a tangy citrus accent. As the fragrance of yuzu reached her nose, Yuiko closed her eyes in bliss.

She'd only sampled one of the nine dishes, and already she felt utterly content.

Working as a nurse meant irregular hours. That, coupled with the fact that she lived alone, meant she rarely managed to enjoy a proper meal. Most of the time she simply picked up a convenience store bento on her way back from the hospital, or ordered udon from a local restaurant.

When she felt like treating herself, she ate at the izakaya on the ground floor of her apartment building. In winter, the menu always featured at least one crab dish, but the crab was reliably flavourless and of uncertain origin. It was an experience that usually left her feeling vaguely melancholic.

She tried the steamed oyster and namafu duck, and found them delicious enough. But the crab had made such an impression on her that they seemed almost ordinary by comparison.

Yuiko filled her cup to the brim with sake, then downed it in one go. At the izakaya she'd used sake to wash away the crab's stale, fishy aftertaste. Now, she realized with a sudden rush of emotion, she was drinking it in order to savour its lingering sweetness.

She slid the now-empty steamer to the rear of the table, then drew the one on the right towards her.

For the beef-tongue stew, served in a small casserole dish, she reached for the spoon wrapped in a paper napkin. The stew was still steaming hot, and the meat, though infused with the two flavours of miso, was lighter than she'd expected – with a clean aftertaste that, again, begged to be chased down with sake.

As she gazed down at the empty gratin dish, a series of words came to mind. Yuiko hastily scribbled them down on the napkin.

'How are you for sake?' asked Nagare, poking his head through the curtain.

Yuiko gave the flask a light shake. 'I think there's a tiny bit left.'

'I'll warm you up another one, then,' said Nagare with a grin. Yuiko smiled back and thanked him.

She was roughly halfway through the meal when it dawned on her that she didn't want to finish it. Instead, she was overwhelmed by the desire to take the rest home, freeze it and savour a little of it every day.

Nagare returned with the flask of warm sake, and Yuiko confessed her wish. He responded with a pained smile.

'It's flattering that you'd want to do that, but . . .'

'It feels wrong to eat all this amazing food in one go. Like I'll drop dead in the morning or something.'

'Now, now – no need to be dramatic.'

'No, I really mean it. It's like I'm tempting fate.'

Noticing that Yuiko wasn't smiling, Nagare tightened his lips. 'Please – just enjoy the food at your own pace.'

'Alright,' replied Yuiko, her eyes glued to the steamer in front of her.

She turned her attention to the fugu, wondering what part of the fish it was. When she tried a bite her first thought, blasphemous as it might be, was that it tasted a bit like chicken breast. It had the same pleasant firmness and was satisfyingly chewy. With the negi and ponzu garnish adding a bright, refreshing edge, it felt like something she could have eaten for ever.

She moved on to the final steamer, and savoured every mouthful.

'Shall I bring that rice through? As there were no fried dishes in the main meal, I've topped it with crab tempura.'

'Oh, I love tempura. Yes, I'll have it now, thanks. Don't want to keep your daughter waiting.'

'There's no rush at all. I'll bring it out in a moment.'

Nagare made his way back into the kitchen. There was only a curtain dividing it from the dining area, which meant she could hear the sizzle of the tempura – and smell the sesame oil it was fried in. Yuiko was already stuffed to bursting, and yet her stomach still rumbled. Tempura had that sort of effect on her.

'I've gone easy on the rice so you'll be able to finish it,' he said, returning with two bowls. 'For the tempura I've used claw meat only. The tsuyu sauce is the darker Tokyo type – personally, I prefer it that way. Sprinkle over some of the powdered sansho pepper if you like. And this is a simple red miso soup with tofu. As I say, take your time – though I always think dishes like this taste best when you guzzle them down.' Nagare grinned and ducked back into the kitchen.

A thin column of steam was rising from the small blue-and-white rice bowl. Yuiko hurriedly removed its lid, then let out a quiet gasp.

When Nagare had mentioned claw meat, she'd expected something like a crab croquette, where the claw was often still attached. Instead, what she found on top of the rice was a thin, round kakiage-style fritter.

How had he even managed to fry it into this shape? The question had barely formed in her mind when it was rendered meaningless by the tempting aromas drifting up from the bowl. Yuiko began wolfing down the dish.

In between bites of the crispy tempura, she practically drank down the sauce-drenched rice, the sweet flavour of the crab meat lingering on her tongue. Yuiko was on the verge of tears. She'd had no idea a simple tempura bowl could ever taste this good.

Pausing occasionally to sip on the tofu miso soup, she demolished the entire dish in three minutes flat. There wasn't a grain of rice left in the bowl.

'Went down well, then?' asked Nagare, arriving at her side with a rustic Mashiko teapot.

'I'm . . . lost for words. You know, I was planning on asking if I could at least take this dish home with me. But before I knew it I'd finished the whole thing.'

'That's what we like to hear. Now, when you've had a moment to digest, I'll show you through to the office.'

When Yuiko had finished her tea, she followed him down the corridor that led to the back of the building, pausing occasionally to gaze admiringly at the photos on the walls. Most of them were of food, but some appeared to capture moments Nagare had shared with his family. Mountains, amusement parks, the seaside . . . it dawned on Yuiko, with a strange satisfaction, that families everywhere always took the same sorts of photos.

Of course, her own photos were different. They stopped when her son reached a certain age. Her heart beat faster at the thought of an impossible photo – one that showed her with him as a young man.

'Koishi will see you now,' said Nagare, opening the door at the end of the corridor.

'Come in!' called Koishi cheerfully. Yuiko bowed to Nagare, then stepped inside.

She sat down, and Koishi slid a form across the low table. Yuiko grinned.

'Something funny?' asked Koishi, frowning slightly.

'Sorry,' said Yuiko, still smiling. 'I spend half my life handing forms out. Feels odd being on the receiving end.'

'Let me guess,' said Koishi, setting a glass of water in front of her. 'Municipal administration?'

'I'm a nurse. We have to give every patient an intake form where they write down what's been bothering them or why they've come.'

'Wow, I'd never have guessed you were a nurse. You look more like one of those glamorous Ginza ladies. Or a model.'

Yuiko flinched slightly at the mention of Ginza, but Koishi didn't seem to notice. 'If you'd seen me twenty-five years ago,' she replied, her lips curling into a faint smile, 'you probably wouldn't be saying that.'

Koishi gazed at her for a moment, then said, 'Well, let's get to it. What dish would you like us to find?'

'Macaroni gratin.'

'From a particular restaurant?'

'Yes. A place in Shizuoka called Tapestry.'

'I'm guessing it's not there any more.'

'Actually, as far as I know, it is.'

'Then why don't you just . . .' Noticing Yuiko's stiff expression, Koishi changed tack. 'Right, there must be a reason why you can't go back there. Which is why you've come to us.'

Yuiko uncrossed her legs. 'I suppose I should tell you the whole story.'

'Whatever you're comfortable sharing,' said Koishi, pen in hand.

'Twenty-five years ago, I got divorced, and my ex-husband got custody of my son Masaya. He was only five at the time. And then—'

'Hang on. Twenty-five years ago would make you, what, thirty-two? And you've lived alone since then?'

'Yes. I've been on my own all this time.'

'Right. Sorry for interrupting. What were you saying about your son?'

'As part of the divorce I agreed never to see Masaya again. In fact, I wasn't in contact with my ex-husband, so I wouldn't have been able to find him even if I'd tried. For all I knew they could have been dead.'

'Sorry to cut in again, but can I ask a delicate question?'

Yuiko lifted her gaze from the table. 'What is it?'

'It's just that with a child that age, it's usually the mother who gets custody – but you agreed never to see him again. Was there a reason?'

'Right,' said Yuiko, crossing her legs again. 'I suppose I need to explain that part, too.'

Koishi set her pen down. 'If it's hard to talk about, I understand. I just wondered.'

'We got divorced because I had an affair. My husband and his mother both insisted that a woman like that had no business raising a child. It was true I'd cheated, so I couldn't exactly argue. They branded me unfit to be a mother.' A pained look flitted across Yuiko's face, followed by one of resignation and, finally, a faint, self-mocking smile.

Koishi frowned and began restlessly clicking her pen. 'I'm not sure how to put this, but . . . doesn't a five-year-old boy need a mother?'

'My mother-in-law was still quite young, and happy to

take on that role. Again, I was the one in the wrong, so I felt like I had no choice but to accept it.'

'It just doesn't sit right with me. Taking a child away from his mother, at that age . . .' Koishi puffed out her cheeks in frustration.

'I didn't want Masaya getting caught up in it all,' explained Yuiko, tilting her gaze towards the ceiling. 'All I wanted was for him to have a safe and happy childhood.'

'Right. Sorry for getting off track. Shall we get back to the gratin?'

'One of the conditions of my divorce was that I leave Tokyo – to keep me from seeing Masaya, I think. I moved to Nagoya and found a position at a hospital in Chikusa. Life began to feel a little empty, so I decided to join a gogyoka poetry group.'

'Gogyoka?'

'As in, "five-line poetry". The idea is that, unlike haiku or tanka, there are no strict rules about syllables. As long as it's five lines long, anything goes. You just express your feelings as they come to you.'

'Sounds fun.'

'It really is. I was hooked right away. We go on trips together, which is always a blast. We choose a theme, write poems during the trip and share them with each other, offering feedback and encouragement. Of course, it isn't just about the poetry. Going for meals, drinking together, sharing stories about our lives – it's really helped ease my loneliness.'

'Wow,' said Koishi, tapping her pen against her head. 'Maybe I should sign up. I could do with something like that in my life.'

'We take trips three or four times a year. Three years ago, in the autumn, we went to Shizuoka.'

'Hmm, Shizuoka – I'm guessing the theme was Mount Fuji?'

'That's right. How did you know?'

Koishi shrugged. 'Hey, this is a detective agency.'

'The trips are always two days long, and include an overnight stay. On the morning of the second day we usually go our separate ways. On this occasion we were staying at a hotel near Shizuoka station. We said goodbye after breakfast as usual, and I went for a stroll around Asama Shrine and Sunpu Castle. Then I got hungry and started looking for somewhere to have lunch.'

'I've never been to Shizuoka,' commented Koishi. 'Famous for tea, isn't it? I'm imagining the smell of it wafting through the air.'

'Yes, there were tea shops all over the place. The streets are all named after old Edo-period businesses – you know, "money changer's street", "dyer's street" and so on – and there's this lovely leafy avenue called Aoba-dori. Anyway, as I was walking past a park, I spotted a cafe. The sign said Tapestry.' An excited gleam had come into Yuiko's eyes.

'Tapestry,' said Koishi, repeating the English word. 'As in one of those cloths you hang on a wall?' She began sketching an illustration in her notebook.

'People your age might not know, but for my generation it's actually music the word brings to mind. There's a Carole King album by that name, see, and I used to be crazy about it. That makes me sound like some connoisseur, but it was my older sister who got me hooked. She's ten years older than me, and I was just a kid at the time – though maybe one who liked to pretend she was a grown-up.'

'Carole King, eh? Can't say I'm familiar. Was this back when people listened to records?'

'Naturally,' said Yuiko, a faraway look coming into her eyes. 'It came in one of those big sleeves. That was partly what I loved about it. Carole sitting there on the windowsill with her jeans and curly hair, one knee up, a big smile on her face and a cat at her side. I remember taking photos with my sister where we'd copy the pose.'

'I'll have to check it out sometime. So, do you think the owner of the cafe was a fan of the album too?'

'I had a feeling he might be. But I couldn't ask.'

'Why, was it too busy?'

'No. I got there before the lunch rush. I was the only customer there.'

'So . . . why didn't you ask him?'

The light in Yuiko's eyes seemed to dim slightly. 'I was too scared.'

'Scared? Of what?'

'The funny thing about being a mother,' murmured Yuiko, tightly pursing her lips, 'is you always recognize the child you brought into this world.'

Koishi gaped at her. 'You don't mean . . .'

'The man brewing coffee was my son, Masaya. I was certain of it,' said Yuiko, staring blankly into space. 'The last time I'd seen him he was five years old, so of course he looked and sounded like a completely different person. But I knew. A mother knows. And I used to play him Carole King songs as lullabies. So I thought maybe . . .'

'What are the chances . . . I'd probably have keeled over on the spot!'

Koishi's attempt at lightening the mood went completely unnoticed. Yuiko was still gazing into the middle distance.

'There were three options for lunch. The daily special, the daily pasta dish and the macaroni gratin. I went straight for the gratin.'

'And that's what you want us to recreate. Right, we're back on track.'

'Sorry,' said Yuiko, turning to face her and bowing slightly. 'Have I been rambling?'

'Not at all,' Koishi bowed back. 'I was the one asking all the questions.'

'Anyway, when I saw that dish on the menu, my heart felt like it might burst. Macaroni gratin was the last meal Masaya and I shared.'

'What do you mean by that, exactly?' asked Koishi, gripping her pen once more.

'It's a bit of a long story.'

'Please. Take your time.'

Yuiko drained her glass of water and went on. 'Once the divorce was settled, and I'd agreed not to see Masaya again, my husband arranged for us to have one final meeting. Just the two of us. It was only half a day, but it felt like a dream. We went to a department store, bought toys, got some juice from a stall. For lunch we went to a Western-style place in Ginza named Candle. At first Masaya wanted the kid's set menu, but I'd already decided: our last meal together would be macaroni gratin.'

'Why that dish in particular?'

'Other Western-style dishes – hamburger steak, say, or deep-fried prawns – felt more like "dad food". But there's something about macaroni gratin that feels . . . motherly, somehow. I got it into my head that, even once I'd disappeared from his life, he might remember me whenever he ate it.'

Koishi nodded. 'Now that you mention it, I think of my own mum whenever I eat it. No idea why, but I do.'

'While I was waiting at Tapestry, the same two questions kept swirling through my mind: had he recognized me? And what was the macaroni going to look like? My heart was racing so badly I thought I might hyperventilate. I finished my water in one gulp, and this young waitress came over to refill it. She was beautiful. I started wondering if she was Masaya's girlfriend. Maybe even his wife. And that got my heart racing all over again.' As she spoke, Yuiko's shoulders began rising and falling as her breathing intensified.

'Can I get you some more water?' asked Koishi, getting to her feet. 'Or tea?'

'Tea would be good, if you don't mind.'

Koishi poured her a cup. 'This is like watching a block-buster. I'm on the edge of my seat . . . But of course, take your time.'

Yuiko sipped her tea, smiling faintly at Koishi's attempt to conceal her impatience to know what happened next. 'I must have only waited fifteen minutes, but it felt like an eternity. Whenever he glanced my way and our eyes met, my heart practically stopped beating.'

Koishi topped up the tea. 'I know what you mean. When my boyfriend cooks me something, I can hardly wait to try it.'

'Ah. Is he a chef?'

'Er, yeah,' said Koishi, her cheeks flushing. 'Something like that.'

'We'd been apart so long that it was almost like setting eyes on an old flame. I kept panicking whenever he looked at me.'

'Did he recognize you too, then? I mean, you are his mother.'

'I don't think so. Like I said, I had some surgery done right after the divorce. My way of starting life over. So I look nothing like the mother Masaya remembers.'

'Oh. But . . . what if he just knew it was you on some instinctive level?'

Yuiko was so caught up in her recollection that she didn't seem to hear this question. 'The very first mouthful was enough to take me back to that meal at Candle.' She gazed up at the ceiling in wide-eyed wonder. 'It was the exact same dish. Piping hot, creamy, and it smelled incredible.'

Koishi glanced up at her. 'I don't mean to spoil the story, but . . . isn't macaroni gratin always like that?'

'Well, yes, but . . . it just tasted so *familiar*,' replied Yuiko without breaking out of her dreamy expression. 'See, macaroni is tricky to get right. You don't want it too firm, but it can't be mushy either. But this was just perfect. It's the same with the béchamel: if you're not careful, it ends up all lumpy, which ruins the texture. This one was rich and velvety. People often cook macaroni gratin with shrimp, but at Tapestry it was with chicken – probably because Masaya has a shellfish allergy. We'd chosen the chicken option at Candle for the same reason. The most important part is the seasoning – and that was spot on too. Just the right amount of salt. All told, it was a perfect match for the dish at Candle.' Yuiko spoke breathlessly, illustrating her description with a series of lively gestures.

'Hang on, I'm struggling to keep up!' chuckled Koishi as she scribbled away. 'Oh, and could you tell me your son's full name?'

'Masaya Ogawa. Ogawa as in "small river". Masaya as in "elegance". So, do you think you'll be able to recreate the dish?'

'This Tapestry place. You said it's still in operation, right?'

'As far as I know, yes.'

'Then we can just go to Shizuoka and try the dish ourselves, can't we? We won't mention your name, of course. We'll pretend to be a regular customer.'

'Well, yes. I suppose that's the only way.'

'In that case, this shouldn't be too tricky.'

Yuiko leaned back into the sofa in relief.

'But what made you want to eat it again now, all of a sudden?' asked Koishi.

'I'm not going to be around for ever, you know. I want to see Masaya more and more with every passing day, but

I'm not allowed. It's a dilemma that torments me daily. This is my one way of being with him.'

'Right. Well, I'll make sure Dad gets right on the case.'

As Koishi led them back to the restaurant, Yuiko glanced at the photos lining the corridor.

'If he can make all these different dishes, then I'm in safe hands,' she commented with a satisfied nod.

'Western food isn't exactly his strong suit, but as long as he can sample the original, he should manage.'

Seeing them return, Nagare rose from his seat at the counter. 'That go alright, then?'

'This one should be a breeze, Dad,' said Koishi, patting him on the back.

Nagare gave her a sharp look. 'Something tells me you might regret saying that.' He turned to Yuiko. 'We usually ask for two weeks. Will that work?'

'Yes, there's no rush. Just let me know the date. My shifts can be a little unpredictable, mind, so I might have to come a day or two later.' Yuiko pulled on her jacket, slung her tote over her shoulder and stepped out of the restaurant.

'Aren't you chilly?' asked Koishi as they followed her out onto the blustery street.

'The cold doesn't bother me,' Yuiko replied with a faint smile. 'It's hot weather I can't stand.'

'Safe travels,' said Nagare. Yuiko bowed briefly in return, then set off down the street.

'It's freezing today,' said Koishi, blowing into her hands as they returned inside.

Nagare unfolded his paper at the counter. 'What's she after, then?'

'Macaroni gratin.'

'From a restaurant?'

'A cafe in Shizuoka.'

'Let me guess. The place closed a long time ago.'

'No. It's still there.'

Nagare peered over his newspaper at Koishi. 'And what – we can just go there and try it for ourselves?'

'Yes. That's what she said.'

'Hmm. That does sound easy.'

'Right? This one should be a walk in the park.'

Nagare's expression tightened. 'There's always a catch, though. I'll have to be careful.'

'Hey, what's that?' asked Koishi, pointing to a paper napkin taped to the kitchen wall.

'I'm not exactly sure. She seems to have scribbled

something down and left it on the table. I was going to give it back to her as she was leaving, but it slipped my mind.'

He folded his newspaper and joined Koishi in peering at the napkin.

'Ah, I know,' she said. 'It's a five-line poem.' She recited:

The memory I search for
Is purest white:
Once more to see
My child's smile
From long ago.

'What's a five-line poem?' asked Nagare.

'A poem written in five lines.'

'Right. Thanks for the insight.'

'It's a hobby of hers. She said it's all about writing what you feel,' said Koishi, smoothing out the napkin. 'Thought I might give it a shot myself.'

'You'll need to work on your handwriting first.'

2

Setsubun was the last day of winter according to the traditional lunar calendar, and yet it came at the start of February, when the cold was at its fiercest. When Yuiko emerged from Kyoto station, a wall of freezing air rose to meet her – just as a friend who lived here had warned her it would.

Yuiko prided herself on her tolerance for cold weather, but even she knew better than to turn up in Kyoto at this time of year without a winter coat.

It was a busy period at the hospital, and a whole ten days had passed since Nagare had contacted her. No doubt the cold had grown even harsher in that time. Yes, she was glad she had dug out the grey tweed coat she hadn't worn in years. Neither Tokyo, where she'd grown up, nor Nagoya, where she'd lived for so long, ever experienced a chill like this.

Walking briskly, and with her coat fastened tight, Yuiko soon arrived at the Kamogawa Diner. She let out a long breath, her shoulders relaxing visibly, then slid open the door.

'Hello again.'

'Ah,' said Koishi, beaming at her. 'Good to see you.'

'Thanks for coming back,' Nagare said, removing his cap as he emerged from the kitchen.

'Sorry it's taken me this long. I had shifts every day last week.'

Nagare smiled in response. 'Not at all – we're here whenever you need us. And it's not like this place ever gets busy.'

'Don't worry,' Koishi whispered in her ear. 'Dad found him.' Yuiko's eyes widened.

'It'll take a moment to prepare, so please bear with me,' said Nagare, before making for the kitchen. Yuiko removed and folded her coat, then set it down on a chair.

'Sorry we don't have a rack,' said Koishi.

'Oh, don't worry. That coat's seen better days.'

'Will you be drinking? I can bring you some wine if you like.'

'Not today, thanks. I want to focus on the flavour of the dish.'

'Some tea, then?' Koishi gave her a meaningful look. 'Perhaps something herbal?'

'Yes, that sounds good.'

Koishi looked visibly relieved as she brought over a selection of teabags. 'We have chamomile, rosehip or lemon balm.'

'Lemon balm, please.'

'And would you like it now, or with the meal?'

'Now, please.'

As Koishi disappeared back into the kitchen, Yuiko glanced around the restaurant. It was only her second visit, and yet again she felt that peculiar nostalgia. This time, it wasn't just the fact that it reminded her of the shokudo eateries she'd been to as a child. It was because she was thinking of Masaya, of how she longed to share this meal with him. She began to feel as though she might turn around to find him standing there, a cheerful grin on his face.

From the kitchen came the aroma of the lemon balm tea. Before she'd even realized what was happening, the refreshing and strangely familiar fragrance had brought a smile to her face.

'I'll leave the pot here,' explained Koishi. 'Just help yourself.' She set down a glass teapot, together with a Minton teacup.

Yuiko squinted with pleasure. 'It smells wonderful. I haven't had herbal tea in a very long time.'

'You didn't order it at Tapestry, then?' asked Koishi, as if confirming something.

'I don't even remember if it was on the menu,' replied Yuiko with a puzzled tilt of her head. 'I only had eyes for the gratin. I think I just ordered an iced coffee.'

'Dad says it'll be a little longer. Please just relax and enjoy your tea in the meantime.'

When Koishi had retreated, Yuiko brought the teacup to her lips.

Had there been herbal tea on the menu at Tapestry? She tried her best to remember, but came up with nothing. Still, Koishi seemed to have been trying to tell her something. Did it have something to do with the gratin? As she inhaled the fragrance of the tea, Yuiko let her mind return to that day at Tapestry.

Now that she thought about it, she did recall a row of teacups, similar to the one she was holding, arranged behind the counter. Yuiko turned the cup in her hand, examining it closely.

She had just drained it and was helping herself to a refill when Nagare appeared and set a red tartan-check placemat in front of her.

'Sorry to keep you waiting. Gratin tastes better when it's baked to order. It'll just be a few more minutes.'

As Yuiko watched him hurry back into the kitchen, the image blurred into the scene at Tapestry.

It needs a while in the oven, so please bear with me.

With these words, the young man walked away from the table, and Yuiko noticed that he had the same slight hunch Masaya had as a child. She remembered telling him to stand up straight on his way to nursery school, though her husband had always insisted it must be hereditary. Seeing him from behind like that was what had well and truly convinced her it was Masaya running the cafe.

Was he doing okay, she wondered. Koishi had said Nagare had 'found him', which she'd taken to mean that Masaya was alive and well at the cafe. But she still felt a lingering unease.

'Here we are,' said Nagare, arriving with a steaming white dish. 'It's hot, so watch you don't burn your tongue.'

'Oh . . .' said Yuiko, twitching her nose over the dish. 'It smells just the same.'

'Please – take your time.'

She waited for Nagare to bow and withdraw to the kitchen, then held her phone directly over the gratin and took a photograph.

The white dish, and inside it the white gratin, its surface baked to a golden crust. It really did look identical to the one she'd eaten at Tapestry that day. She remembered the placemat being red, too. Whether its tartan pattern was the same, she couldn't say – but if Nagare had gone all the way to Tapestry to recreate the meal, that seemed likely. Yuiko scooped up a spoonful of macaroni, blew gently on it then brought it to her mouth.

As she slowly chewed, a reassuring warmth spread through her. Yes, this was it. Her eyes closed in rapture.

It wasn't the meal at Tapestry she was remembering. It was Masaya, sitting across from her at Candle. It was the heartbreak of losing him, even if she only had herself to blame. It was the sensation of being wrenched in two as she tried to enjoy their final moments together.

Masaya had pouted as he peered down at the dish, disappointed at being served this plain white gratin instead of one of the colourful kid's lunches. Yuiko hadn't hurried him. Instead, she'd dug her spoon into her own gratin and ate it as he watched. She made a show of savouring the taste, then scrunched her face into a silly smile. That was when Masaya reluctantly reached for his spoon.

It's hot, so mind you don't burn your tongue!

At these words from the waitress Masaya had nodded slightly, then puffed repeatedly on his first spoonful.

Finally, he had slid the spoon into his mouth. He had chewed once, twice, three times, four times. It was only after the fifth chew that Masaya had looked at her – and beamed.

Yuiko opened her eyes, gathered another spoonful and savoured the taste once again.

It really was identical. She was at Candle, and she was at Tapestry. The two were blurring together in her mind. Here, in this restaurant, the two memories had fused into one.

Even as she marvelled at the strangeness of it all, Yuiko's spoon never stopped moving. In no time at all, she had demolished the gratin.

Clink. As if he'd been waiting for the sound of the spoon landing on the empty dish, Nagare stepped through the curtain.

'Well? How was it?'

'That,' replied Yuiko, dabbing at her mouth with a white handkerchief, 'was the gratin I ate at Tapestry. The very same one.'

Nagare looked visibly relieved. 'Glad to hear it.'

'So . . . did you just go there and ask for the recipe?' Yuiko knew this sounded a little insulting to Nagare's skills as a detective, but she had to ask.

'Oh, I'm not quite that brazen. No, I just ate it. Once

wasn't enough, but after trying it a second time, I had a pretty decent idea how it was made.'

'That was all it took? Incredible.'

'Just doing my job,' said Nagare with a hint of pride.

'Do you . . . think I could make it myself?'

Nagare set a sheet of paper in front of her. 'I've written it all down for you. There aren't any fancy ingredients. Just get the measurements and timing right and it should come out exactly the same.'

'Thank you so much,' replied Yuiko, carefully folding the paper into quarters.

'I should probably tell you what happened at the cafe.'

Yuiko nodded eagerly, then gestured at the chair opposite her own.

'Thanks,' said Nagare, removing his cap and sitting down. Koishi brought over a fresh pot of tea, then stood behind him to listen.

'Just imagine. A man my age shows up two days in a row, asking for the macaroni gratin. Anyone would find that a little odd. On the second day, just after I'd finished, the owner came over and said, "Big fan of macaroni, then?"'

Yuiko leaned forward eagerly. 'What did you tell him?'

'Well, a certain habit from my days in the police kicked in,' continued Nagare with a wry smile. 'Stake a place out for too long and people start to get suspicious. If they work out why you're really there, you might as well hand in your badge. So you learn to make up excuses. I told him it reminded me of a restaurant my mother took me to as a child. That it brought back memories.'

'And what did Masa— sorry, I mean, the owner,' said Yuiko breathlessly. 'What did he say to that?'

'Masaya Ogawa told me he knew exactly what I meant. And he reached out to shake my hand.'

As Nagare handed her a business card bearing the name, tears welled in Yuiko's eyes.

'I knew it,' she murmured. 'He remembers.'

Nagare gave Yuiko a moment to gather herself. When he eventually spoke, it was in a low voice. 'But there's something else I should tell you.'

Yuiko glanced up at him, a shadow passing over her face. Koishi, still standing behind Nagare, was staring at the ceiling.

'He told me it was his father who had taken him.'

Now Yuiko's expression clouded over completely. Koishi let out a deep sigh.

'He said his father used to take him to an old Western-style restaurant in Ginza for the chicken macaroni gratin, and that the version he serves is a recreation of that beloved dish.' Nagare spoke slowly, as though gauging her reaction.

'His . . . father . . .' said Yuiko in a low, absent voice. Her heart seemed to have wandered somewhere far away.

'It seems Masaya loved the gratin at Candle so much that he pestered his father to take him back.'

Yuiko winced with frustration. After all these years, she found herself wishing she'd never told her ex-husband the name of that restaurant. He had stolen and tainted a memory that was supposed to belong to her and her son alone.

She gave Nagare a probing look. 'You're sure he said Ginza?'

Nagare nodded silently in response. Then he dealt her another blow. 'About the name of the cafe – Tapestry, I mean . . .'

Yuiko steeled herself and met his gaze.

'It was actually inspired by the teacups.' Nagare was looking at the Minton cup.

'The . . . teacups?' repeated Yuiko, lifting the cup in her hand.

'It's a design known as Haddon Hall, based on the tapestries that once hung in an English castle of that name. Masaya was so fond of it he named his cafe after it.'

'Right . . . Of course,' said Yuiko, nodding over and over as if to convince herself. 'Silly of me to think a child his age would even remember the music I played him.'

For Koishi, listening to her father report these findings was one of the toughest experiences of her entire career as a food detective. She felt as though she were watching Yuiko be pounded by a series of increasingly brutal waves, each of which shattered another of the fragile hopes she had carried over the years. Instead of helping her, they were rubbing salt into an open wound.

The whole point of recreating a dish was to help the client find a sort of peace. Nostalgia was part of the process, but it was usually balanced by a quiet optimism about the future. The client might feel remorse for the past, but it was always accompanied by the sense that things would be easier, or at least different, from now on.

Even if Yuiko had been hasty in her assumptions, couldn't they at least have spared her the truth?

'Still . . .' she murmured, 'I suppose I'm still the one who set all this in motion. I mean, I introduced him to that gratin. Then he grew to love it, and now he's serving it in a cafe in Shizuoka. All because I took him to that restaurant.' With tears brimming in her eyes again, Yuiko was doing her best to hold herself together.

'Ah, yes,' said Nagare. 'There's one other thing I meant to tell you.' Both Yuiko and Koishi waited with bated breath for him to go on. He tapped at a tablet, then set it down on the table. 'Does this look familiar?'

'Wait,' said Yuiko, leaning in to inspect the photo on the screen. 'That's . . .'

'The coaster you wrote on at Tapestry, I believe?'

Yuiko nodded in astonishment.

'It *was* you, then,' said Nagare.

'Where did you even find this?' asked Yuiko, reaching for the tablet.

'It was framed on the wall of the cafe.'

'. . . Framed?'

'That's right. Masaya said a customer had left it behind. At first he thought it was just a casual doodle, but then he realized it was a poem – and one he found oddly encouraging. So he framed it and hung it on the wall.'

'Oh my,' said Yuiko, her cheeks reddening. 'How embarrassing.'

'He reads these five lines aloud every morning before starting work. And whenever he feels like giving up, he goes back and reads them again.'

A gleam came back into Yuiko's eyes as she gazed at the display.

'But . . . how did you know it was mine?'

'You left this behind last time,' said Nagare, as Koishi handed her the paper napkin bearing the five-line poem. 'The handwriting was the same, so I put two and two together. Plus, it's not often you see a coaster framed on a wall. I'm glad I asked him about it.'

'It's a habit of mine,' said Yuiko, smiling shyly as she folded the napkin into a neat square. 'Whenever an idea comes to me, I just have to get it down.'

'Childhood memories are always a little hazy,' Nagare

went on, gazing steadily at her. 'If you ask me, what's important isn't who Masaya remembers taking him to that restaurant. It's that he's grown up into a charming young man. And that after all this time, you've managed to reconnect with him.'

Koishi nodded in agreement. 'It's the same with my own mum. I don't actually remember much about her as a person. It's the things she said that have stayed with me.'

Yuiko took a moment to dwell on Koishi's words, then smiled up at the pair. 'Thank you, really. I'm truly grateful for everything you've done.'

'We're just happy to have helped,' said Nagare, returning her smile.

'If it hadn't been for this, I'd probably have been stuck in the past for ever. Chasing old memories, even though there's no going back.'

'Time waits for no one, as they say, and there's no changing the past. All we can do is try and make each day count.'

'You're absolutely right,' said Yuiko, her expression tightening with resolve. 'I'll carry those words with me.'

'I hope I don't sound preachy. The truth is, it's a lesson I'm still trying to learn myself.'

'I really can't thank you enough.' Yuiko stood and bowed to them from the waist.

Nagare smiled. 'Finding people's food is our job. When there's a clue that might matter, we don't tend to miss it.'

Koishi handed her a slip of paper with their bank details and asked her to pay whatever seemed fair. Yuiko promised to make the transfer as soon as she was back in Nagoya.

'Take care on the way home,' said Koishi. 'Especially in this cold.'

As Yuiko stepped outside, a tabby cat scampered over. 'Ooh, you chubby little thing!' she exclaimed, squatting to pet the animal. 'Is it yours?'

'We've named him, which *I* think makes him ours,' explained Koishi, shooting Nagare a look. 'Drowsy, we call him.'

'Well, he's obviously eating well. I just hope he's getting enough exercise!' Yuiko rubbed the cat's belly, then got to her feet. She began walking westwards down the street, but Nagare's voice stopped her in her tracks.

'Masaya said he wanted to find the woman who left the coaster. You know, so he could thank her. I told him I had an idea who the author might be, and that I'd let her know. He seemed very pleased about that. Of course, what happens next is entirely up to you.' He bowed to her. Yuiko returned the gesture, then set off, walking briskly towards the station. Soon she had vanished from view.

'*Dad*,' snapped Koishi all of a sudden.

'What is it now?'

'Why didn't you tell me about that poem on the coaster? I was barely holding it together back there.'

'Oh. Guess it slipped my mind.' Nagare strolled calmly back into the shop. Koishi trailed after him, still fuming.

'Do you have *any* idea how upset I was?'

'No need to make a fuss,' said Nagare, settling at the counter with his newspaper. 'Anyway, I've told you everything now.'

'Oh, sure . . . I still don't even know how the poem went!'

Koishi swiped away at Nagare's tablet, searching for the photo of the coaster.

'Try the folder labelled "Tapestry",' said Nagare without looking up.

'Ah, here we are. "*Darling child / White as snow / Soft as cotton / May you follow your heart / Wherever it takes you.*" Wow. Isn't that nice? She really did put her feelings straight onto the page.' Koishi hugged the tablet to her chest and sighed. 'I wish I had someone to call me "darling".'

'Oh, but you do,' said Nagare, glancing at the portrait of Kikuko on the family altar.

'Right, I guess I do. Thanks, Mum.'

Koishi kneeled in front of the altar and pressed her hands together.

Nagare silently positioned himself at her side. He glanced sideways at her for just a moment, then lowered his head in prayer.

THE KAMOGAWA FOOD DETECTIVES

What's the one dish you'd do anything to taste just one more time?

Down a quiet backstreet in Kyoto exists a very special restaurant. Run by Koishi Kamogawa and her father, Nagare, the Kamogawa Diner treats its customers to wonderfully extravagant meals. But that's not the main reason to stop by . . .

The father–daughter duo have started advertising their services as 'food detectives'. Through ingenious investigations, they are capable of recreating dishes from their customers' pasts – dishes that may well hold the keys to unlocking forgotten memories and future happiness.

From the widower looking for a specific noodle dish that his wife used to cook to a first love's beef stew, the restaurant of lost recipes provides a link to the past – and a way to a more contented future.

OUT NOW!

THE RESTAURANT OF LOST RECIPES

Tucked away down a Kyoto backstreet lies the extraordinary Kamogawa Diner. Running this unique establishment are a father–daughter duo who serve more than just mouth-watering feasts.

The pair have reinvented themselves as 'food detectives', offering a service that goes beyond traditional dining. Through their culinary sleuthing, they reconstruct beloved dishes from the memories of their customers, creating a connection to cherished moments from the past.

Among those who seek an appointment is a one-hit wonder pop star, finally ready to leave Tokyo and give up on her singing career, who wants to try the tempura that she once ate to celebrate her only successful record. Another diner is a budding Olympic swimmer, who desires the bento lunch box that his estranged father used to make him.

The Kamogawa Diner doesn't just serve meals – it revives lost recipes and rekindles forgotten memories. It's a doorway to the past through the miracle of delicious food.

OUT NOW!

THE MENU OF HAPPINESS

Nostalgic and heartwarming, The Menu of Happiness *features more uplifting tales from Kyoto's Kamogawa Food Detectives as they recreate favourite dishes from their customers' pasts.*

Welcome to the Kamogawa Diner, where every meal is a mystery ready to be solved. This unique establishment is run by a father–daughter duo who offer more than just mouth-watering meals. They act as 'food detectives', delving into the past to produce nostalgia-infused dishes for their hungry clientele.

Among the patrons is a once-renowned pianist whose promising career was marred by a self-inflicted injury. She longs to taste the yakisoba shared with the only man she ever truly loved. The diner also welcomes a man haunted by shadows of regret. His mind races back to the gyoza served by the parents of a lover he once jilted, as he seeks understanding and, perhaps, forgiveness.

The Kamogawa Diner doesn't just serve food – it revives the essence of forgotten recipes and rejuvenates cherished memories. Each dish is a portal to the past, serving not just sustenance but solace and reconnection through the miracle of delicious food.

The Menu of Happiness follows on from *The Kamogawa Food Detectives* and *The Restaurant of Lost Recipes.*

OUT NOW!